A Hot Summer

A QUEEN NOVEL

DEDICATION

This book is dedicated to all the readers around the world who cherish a good read, and to all the people who aren't afraid to venture off into different worlds. A special thank you to S. Pillars & T. Campbell Jackson for inspiring me to believe in this project for more than just a hobby, and to see the bigger picture. To S. Lord, D. Teague, and E.A. Brown let the success of this work show you that there are no ceilings!

Table of Contents

ACKNOWLEDGMENTS

All of the readers who sampled the book before publishing and to the
entire Hot Summer Pre Release Book Club: T Campbell Jackson,
T Washington Frazier, S. Lord
E. Crowley, S. Pillars, K. Rule, L. Taylor-Shade, T. Thomas, A. Williams

C. Madison- Graphic Designer (cover)

1 SUMMER

Huhhh...this pussy of mine always seems to get me in trouble. It's not a time that I can remember where I ain't done some type of dumb shit to put myself in a fucked up position.

Now, I'm the cause of a love triangle gone badly and somehow, I still can't help myself. I'm still addicted to the soft touches to my pussy and any type of cum fest I can get my hands on. It's a fucked up weakness, but it's who I am.

My mother used to say before she had me she was hot, while she was pregnant with me she was hot, so when she had me she named me Summer.

That's who I am, Summer, a fucking hot ass Summer.

I'm addicted to niggas with money and being fucked real good. The combination is a mixture for a shit show and I'm usually involved in one.

I can't say that I haven't lived up to my name but, shit, that's the way it is growing up in the hood. There ain't nothing more irresistible than a fine ass hood nigga.

It's not like I had a great example set for me, especially considering my role model. My mama made is all about money, securing the bag. I was groomed at a young age to do that.

It wasn't about traditional goals like education or jobs, but more about using my looks to get ahead.

Shit, somedays I didn't even have food, but Mama made sure I looked the part. She made sure the message was clear, get a dope boy.

When I was younger I used to despise the way I looked. I mean I was 11 years old, tall, fair skinned with long curly black hair. I hated my eyes, they were big and green with a slant. People would always ask me what I was mixed with. Shit, I didn't know. That was probably the worst part.

How could you know who your Daddy was when your Mama either didn't know or just wouldn't tell you? I'm sure it was one of her many Johns.

I used to compare my looks to the Johns I'd see, hoping to see a resemblance. A lot of her Johns were regulars so I would see them two, three times a week.

It became too many to narrow down and I soon stopped trying to figure it out.

Mama, although she was a coke head, was highly desired and always booked. She prioritized her Johns according to financial status.

I had full lips and a slender nose. I wasn't a petite girl, but I definitely wasn't fat which made my hourly glass shape more noticeable. It was always difficult to find clothes because I had a thin waist with a big butt.

One thing Mama made a priority was my appearance. She would always buy me fine clothes from all of the latest labels. I didn't understand it then, but later in life I got it. It was all a part of her grooming techniques.

Mama wasn't concerned with making sure I ate so much, but she was sober long enough to make sure she kept me up on my appearance.

She was always consumed with my appearance and reminded me constantly of the beauty that I carried.

She would often scold me about my naive attitude about the way I looked and always warned me of the envy my beauty would bring.

I wasn't allowed to have girlfriends. All the girls at school hated me anyway so it didn't matter and the boys' only interest was feeling on me. I got used to it. I mean, after a while it wasn't too bad.

I learned to use it to my advantage by the age of 15. By that time I had a fat ass, slim stomach, and a nice titty cup.

Elementary school were my hell days. I came to school to escape the nightmares of home. Me and Mama lived in the hood in a 1 bedroom apartment. It was a shit hole.

We had an old television that didn't have color and we ain't have no cable. Mama took the room and gave me an air mattress for the front room. She used to tell me that she needed the room in case she was entertaining a private client.

Client, like she was a business woman or some shit. The Johns were always dressed well, mostly suits, and their colognes were very present even after they

2

left. They wore expensive jewelry and sometimes very noticeable wedding rings.

I didn't even understand why the hell they'd want to come to our house to fuck. I'm sure there was some hotel accessible.

But hell, where were their goddamn standards?

They were fucking a whore, eating her pussy, and sometimes her ass with an entire family at home. All of this in a damn house the size of a large room. You could practically stretch your legs from the living room to the kitchen.

Our wood kitchen table was collected from the sidewalk after one of our neighbors got put out, and we had two old yellow kitchen chairs with rips in the leather.

Our refrigerator was a nasty beige color and, for the most part, all you would really find in there was a half-gallon of milk and some baking soda. Sometimes it was some sort of half-eaten restaurant food and a half drank beer. I mostly survived off Ramen Noodles and read books from the school library to escape from my shitty reality.

Most times I was at home alone because Mama was on dates with her Johns. That shit always blew my mind. What kind of Johns take a coked out whore on a date? Where were their wives? Didn't they have any kind of conscious?

And if Mama was home, she usually brought her John with her and was not shy about fucking him anywhere in the house, no matter where I was.

Most times I was required to watch the fucking sessions to "learn" how to secure the bag. She would say, "Summer, watch me" while she would be unbuckling her John's belt buckle; "You gotta learn how to suck dick like this so you ain't gotta be broke. You gone find you a nigga that's gone take care of you and you gone keep him, train him, by sucking his dick like this."

I learned at an early age that the pussy and the mouth of a woman controls everything. A woman's mouth was made for more than just talking.

There I was 12 years old, watching my mother- sucking away, as the dick stood fully erected. She would play with the balls of some of her Johns, licking them and explaining all of her actions and their reactions as if the shit was a school lesson.

Sometimes she would play with her own pussy while she was doing it. She would tell me that the only way I would know how to teach someone to make me feel good was if I knew how to make myself feel good.

The tripped out part about it was the John's never stopped moaning long enough to care that a fucking kid was watching them get their dick sucked.

That's some crazy shit, but that's how I learned the game.

Very early in life I started playing with my pussy. I initially would use my fingers, rubbing on my clit, finding relaxation in the satisfaction that my self-created orgasms gave me.

Eventually, my fingers weren't enough. I craved the type of satisfaction I would see my Mama experience when she would find that spot upright on a John. It was a place that I could never bring myself to just sticking my fingers in my pussy.

One day when Mama was out, I went searching in her room and found a drawer that was full of toys. I had no idea what half of the toys were or how they worked, so I took the easiest thing. It was a small silver vibrator called The Bullet.

Once I tried it I was hooked. I spent countless nights laying on my air mattress alone in my house rubbing The Bullet up and down my clit, massaging my titties, moving my bottom up and down in sync with The Bullet until I would explode from an orgasm.

I would do it multiple times, mainly whenever I had a dream or after watching Mama and a John together. The moans would turn me on and it was so difficult to wait until they were gone to be alone and pleasure myself.

I had never been touched by a man, so the feeling that I gave myself was the closest thing I had experienced to sex.

Sometimes I would grab a Zane novel and lose myself in the fictional world, stopping multiple times to call my body to orgasm. I was addicted to the orgasm and at one point it became all I could ever think about.

2 MAMA

Mama was five feet five inches tall. She was fair skinned with long silky black hair. She had green eyes just like mine, but hers were big and beautiful. Mama's lips were full and always glossy. She had perfect perky titties, a slim tummy, and a big booty. You couldn't tell she had a kid. There was no marks to prove it. You also couldn't tell that Mama was a coke head prostitute. She was beautiful, like one of them damn models you meet from the Penthouse magazine. She had perfect teeth and deep dimples. I couldn't figure out for shit how somebody so beautiful ended up living like she was.

Sometimes when she would come in without her John she would say, "Summer, come lay with me". For a small moment I would feel a connection, like she was my mother. She would tell me the stories of her youth. Some of the stories were good, some were bad. I'd forget about all the fucked up shit I saw her do. She was just my Mama. Even though she was high, I had the chance to pretend that we were a normal family and I lived for those moments.

On the night of my fifteenth birthday she came in high and she sat on my air mattress; she started to sob. This was a pretty usual night with her so at first I paid her no mind. She motioned me to come over and lay with her. "Summer, come lay with me", she said through her sniffles. I want to tell you of your grandparents.

That night she told me the story of our family. She had never talked about her parents and I didn't even know if she had siblings. I didn't know anything about where my Mama came from. I didn't even understand why she chose that particular night to tell me. She had waited fifteen years to tell me about a family that I had longed for. I wasn't going to miss the opportunity to learn about Mama's family and definitely not the chance to possibly find out who my Daddy was.

She told me that she came from a wealthy family. Her parents were loaded apparently. My grandmother had met my grandfather when she was sixteen years old and he was twenty five. My grandfather was a man of money and he had paid my grandmother's family for my grandmother's hand in marriage. The two had been together since.

 Mama described her cars (a teenager with more than one car) in great detail. Mama's father had bought her first car at the age of twelve and another at fifteen. She had also gone to an Ivy League prep school and had lots of friends.

I could see the twinkle in her eyes as she talked about how well she always dressed. She said it was something that her mother required from her and her Daddy enjoyed allowing her to do after spending time with her alone.

Mama told me the stories of her extensive wardrobe that was in a room of its own on her own wing of the house. Her family owned a mansion in one of the most prestigious neighborhoods in the city. The mansion sat on a hill in a gated community with the next house not even in walking distance. Mama talked about the staff in her old home; two butlers, a staff of housekeepers, a chef, and the personal trainer that she was required to work out with every day.

She described the beauty of her mother, my grandmother. Mama told me that her mother was a retired supermodel. She was light skinned, had jet black waist length hair with a perfect wave, and her body was that of a slender build. She was in excellent shape with perfect perky titties, a super flat belly, and a perfect shaped ass. She worked out every day and was consumed with her appearance. Grandmother was never seen without looking perfect, not even by my mother. "She walked as if she were gliding on clouds", Mama said, "And she was loved by every man that ever laid eyes on her."

Mama talked about how my grandmother's graceful ageing made her grow less appealing to my grandfather; and although my grandmother was still very beautiful, perfect actually, my grandfather desired someone younger. Mama had little to say about my grandfather in that moment, except for the fact that I looked exactly like him. I could tell that it pained her to speak of him. My question didn't leave her much choice though.

"Mama, why did you leave a home like that to live here?" She told me that she had been on her own since she was sixteen.

She said, "One day, in the late summer, when I was sixteen years old, I decided to tell my mother that my father was fucking me and had been fucking me since I was nine years old." I was definitely caught off guard with that response. I mean, what the fuck?! Your own damn Daddy was fucking you?

"I didn't want to tell her. I didn't have a choice. In my heart I knew that my mother knew anyway. I saw it in her eyes and I felt it in her growing hatred for me. She already knew that her husband was taking her child every night but shit was going to get very real. She was going to actually see it, sooner or later." My Mama's words ripped through me like a sword. How could her mother allow her Daddy to fuck her?! What kind of mother didn't protect their daughter?

And I didn't know what she meant about seeing it sooner or later but I could tell that it wasn't the time to press for information. Mama was one of those people that would tell you what she wanted when she wanted to tell you. So, although I had a million questions racing through my mind, I didn't interrupt her, I just let her talk.

"I started developing at a young age and my Daddy started sitting me on his lap more". I mean, he had always held me so I was pretty used to it. I was Daddy's girl, he loved me and I loved him. But as I got older and he would sit me on his lap and it always made his dick hard. I was too young to understand it then. He would tell me that he loved me more often and he started kissing me on my lips, instead of my cheek like normal, when I was about nine years old."

"I couldn't understand why my Mama suddenly acted as if she hated me. My mother was no longer the nurturing loving mother she had always been to me. She was cold. My mother wanted me gone! She tried sending me off to boarding school but Daddy would not have me out of his sight. He ignored Mama's demands and the decision was made that I would remain at home. Then one night when Mama went to bed Daddy came in to read me a bedtime story, like every night, but this wasn't like the other nights. He brought me a present with him."

I could feel my Mama, a woman that I'd never seen scared of anything, shudder. She recalled," He said, Maddy, put this on for Daddy. Shit, I didn't know, I did what I was told. I went into my bathroom, opened the bag, and put on what I thought was a grown up gown, the kind that I'd seen my mother in before."

"When I opened the door to the bathroom Daddy met me there. He picked me up and laid me on my bed. He started rubbing his hands on my nipples. I told him, Daddy, I don't like that, please don't do that, but it didn't seem like he heard me. He kept telling me that I was so beautiful and I reminded him of my mother when she was younger. The next thing I know my Daddy, the man that I loved, put his fingers in my pussy Summer. I cried out in pain but he didn't care. He didn't stop. That night changed me."

"For a couple years Daddy would come in, only at night, and he would put his fingers in my pussy and take them out; put them back in again and take them out. I would watch in disgust as he licked his fingers and I would cry while he was doing it. At first it hurt. It hurt so badly and then one day it didn't. I began to close my eyes and it made me feel so good."

"When I was twelve it was no longer just happening at night. Daddy would come into my room whenever he had time, mostly after school, and he would finger my pussy. He would finger my pussy and I would close my eyes, imagining he was someone else, while I grabbed his hand and helped him finger it."

"When I turned fifteen Daddy licked my pussy for the first time. Summer, I didn't want it to feel good, I swear to god. I hated him, but somehow my pussy erupted in his mouth and I heard myself moaning".

"He would lick and suck on my pussy often and I started to look forward to him licking my pussy. I looked forward to the feeling he gave my pussy. Only he could make it feel the way he did. When I fingered my pussy on the days that Daddy missed his visits, I wasn't satisfied. I needed more."

"And when he would lick my pussy I would imagine he was someone else, not my goddamn Daddy. I wanted him to make my pussy feel good and he seemed to be happy doing that. He had started buying me very expensive gifts too. The gifts weren't the usual. I went from being my Daddy's child to becoming his fucking girlfriend and my mother knew it. She never stopped it, she let him have me, any way he wanted. She hated me, instead of him."

"When I was sixteen Daddy came in as normal, and I was dying to have his mouth on my pussy. My pussy was sending all kinds of tingling sensations and I needed to get it out; but this time he didn't eat my pussy. He didn't finger my pussy either, he got on top of me and he fucked my pussy. I cried out in pain, in anguish; but he didn't stop. The pain didn't last long, it quickly became pleasure. He kissed my neck and my ear, and sucked on my titties."

"Maddy, you're so beautiful, he whispered in my ear. I wanted him and I moaned. I didn't want it to be him, but I wanted him. It seemed like it lasted forever and we were not quiet. We both moaned in passion, I bit his bottom lip softly. My pussy erupted first, the flow from the depths of my soul and Daddy last, and it was quiet. Daddy got up, wiped himself off with my sheet and left."

"My mother told me I was a fucking liar and I was trying to take my goddamn Daddy from her". "They kicked me out with no money, nowhere to go, and disowned me. It was the last time I saw my parents." I looked over and Mama was already asleep.

3 REINA

Shit pretty much changed for me when I was 15. Learning about where my Mama came from and leaving elementary school was just the beginning.

That was my first year of high school. I was always a smart kid so I kept straight A's. It still didn't get me anywhere. I mean what was I to do, I was living in the hood with a coked out prostitute mother, and seriously addicted to orgasms.

My options were limited. I wasn't interested in college or making friends. I had only one interest, securing the bag.

The first day I walked into the high school I knew shit was about to get interesting. I had suddenly gone from being the little girl who just wanted to die because of the grown up body and the long curly hair with the stupid big green slanted eyes, to being the most desired girl in the school. I had fully embraced my body and was well aware of my beauty and how to use it to my full advantage. I turned heads when I walked down the hallways and I knew it. You could practically see the high school boy's dicks protruding from their pants as I glided down the hallways with a smirk.

None of that mattered, I wasn't interested in any of the high school boys. I knew better than to get caught up with a high school boy with no money. Most of Mama's lessons stuck with me. Every day she would say, "Summer, don't bring no broke ass nigga to this house. You go get you one of them dope boys." I knew better than to even think for a moment that I would ever be a normal high school girl. And I had one focus, getting the dope boy.

Freshman year was also when I met Reina. Reina is my best friend. She is 5'4, light skinned with a slender figure. She got bigger titties than mine, but a smaller booty. Her core is ripped, flat and six packed with a diamond belly ring displayed in the middle of the vines from her tattoo that run into her pussy area.

She has a nose piercing and wears a small nose ring. Reina is gorgeous, one of the only other women I've ever seen almost as gorgeous as Mama. She has a round face with almond shaped hazel eyes. She has long hair that has some of the deepest waves I've ever seen. If I needed to wear a weave, I'd definitely want the hair to be like hers. Her hair is copper which is perfectly matched with her smooth, beautiful skin tone.

She has the dopest full body tattoo that I've ever seen and because of her complexion, the color scheme is popping. It is impossible to not stare at it. The tattoo is of a jungle and there are birds, trees, and animals in it.

She's two years older than me but she acts so much older. She was one of the only bitches that didn't give me envious looks when passing in the hallway and was as well dressed, if not better, as me.

She would usually walk past me and smile. At first sight Reina looked no nonsense and always in complete control. The boys gawked at her, afraid to make a step, but they licked their lips as she walked down the halls. She seemed completely unbothered and unentertained by them, as was I. She didn't stay in her own lane, Reina owned the freeway.

About a week into the school year during lunch, she motioned me over to sit with her and eat my lunch. The motion did not seem like a question, more of a demand. But I walked over out of curiosity. She was mysterious and appealing and I felt drawn to her. The table was empty, besides her, and it didn't seem that anyone who walked past dared to attempt to sit there.

When I sat down, without looking up from her meal, she politely said, "Summer, is it? You're not from around here are you?" I chuckled at her and responded, "I don't know what makes you think that, I live on the next block over. Where you from?"

Reina looked up at me and smiled. "You're dope. I think we should be friends. I can show you around the school. I pretty much know everybody that's anybody and everybody knows me."

We chopped it up for the rest of the lunch hour. I told her about Mama and she told me about what she remembered about her mother before she died of an overdose.

Reina didn't talk much about her father, other than he was a shit father and she pretty much was raised in foster homes until the age of fifteen when she moved out on her own.

I wondered how she managed to take care of herself since she never talked about having a job. She told me that she lived on the east end; and I thought to myself, how the fuck could she afford to live on the fucking east end at seventeen?!

That's where Mama was from, the east end. I didn't press for information. Reina seemed very strategic in what information she allowed me to have and more interested in learning about me.

After that we were pretty much together inseparable. Reina drove so sometimes we would leave for lunch and come back. Sometimes we would just leave. Reina taught me about my beauty and how to use it at another level. She was so strategic, dope, and very businesslike.

I was always well dressed, but it was now a requirement of Reina's to hang out. "Summer, if you ever ain't got nothing to wear you call me. Don't fucking show up in no shit you already wore in the same fucking year."

We spent a lot of time together. Reina's lessons reminded me a lot of Mama's lessons.

One day I was skipping classes because I was just too tired to deal with the fucking work of paying attention. I didn't get any sleep the night before; Mama had a John and they were at it forever!

When they left I played with my pussy multiple times and worked my bullet to pull multiple orgasms from my body. It lasted until the early morning and I was super exhausted the next day.

I decided that I was going to chill out in the gym and smoke a joint to relax my mind.

While I was sitting in the gym Reina walked in. She came right up to me and asked me to hit the joint.

We got to chopping it up about the school and life in general. I was telling her about Mama's John the night before and my irritation from the lack of sleep caused by the aggravating moans of them both. I left out my afterward activities.

Halfway through the conversation, she stopped and asked, "Summer, you ever fucked anybody yet?" Shit I didn't want to look like no fool so I lied and told her I did.

She just started laughing and told me I was lying. Then we were laughing together. Reina knew me damn near better than myself. She knew that I had never fucked any of them niggas that I had wrapped around my finger and that I was, low key, scared to.

As we were finishing up the joint, Reina said, "Summer, come here, I want you to go lay on that gym mat". I was like, "Reina, why the fuck do you want me to lay on a gym mat fool?"

She said, "Because I want to fuck you. I'm going to kiss your lips and then move down to your perfectly shaped titties.

Then I'm going to take my tongue and lick your belly, licking and kissing it until I get to your pussy. When I get to your pussy I'm going to lick it slowly, stopping long enough to bite your ass cheeks.

Then I'm going to gently bite the inside of your thighs and continue to lick your pussy while I finger you in your ass until you cum in my mouth."

I was shocked, scared, yet I was aroused.

I replied, "Chill Reina, I ain't with that shit. I like niggas".

She grabbed my hands and led me to the gym mat. Then she laid me down and responded, "So do I" and pulled my legs open gently.

The next thing I knew she was fingering me and I was moaning. She began to kiss me in my mouth. Her lips were so soft and I didn't exactly know what was happening. I wasn't sure what was happening with my pussy but it was like nothing I'd ever felt before and I knew that I needed to feel it more.

The gym was dimly lit. It didn't even matter that the mat was hard because every sensual touch from her sent a chill through my body. I had never had anyone suck my titties so good, shit I had never had anyone suck my titties period.

As she kissed my stomach and rubbed my titties, I could feel my nipples get hard the closer she got to my pussy. And then she was there. She sucked and kissed my pussy like she had been in a relationship with it for years and had been away. I moaned, she moaned.

I could see her playing with her pussy. I wanted her. I wanted to kiss her pussy, to give her the feeling she was giving me.

I began to shake. I didn't know what the feeling was that had me in another dimension. Even my bullet had never made me feel the way that I felt in that moment.

QUEEN

I started trying to move her head but she wasn't budging. I was about to explode and I didn't know what would come out. I didn't want to be embarrassed.

Reina still didn't move, she just kept going, as if she was unaware of my pushing. Her moaning was turning me on and she just keep putting her warm, soft tongue into my clit.

It felt like it was melting inside, like she was tongue kissing it. Why was she making me feel so good? She stuck two fingers in my ass and she pushed them in forcefully, but the slight pain on top of the warm feeling from her tongue on my pussy gave way to an irresistible sensation.

Suddenly I felt my pussy contract and my toes curl. I let out a squeak of excitement, and I was wet. It was pouring out of me and Reina continued to lick as if she didn't know. I found myself whispering, "Oh Reina, Jesus."

She came up and she laid next to me. She said, "Summer, did you like that?" I excitedly told her that I did.

She said, "I want you to remember that. Anybody can make your pussy feel good. Don't get attached to these niggas. We're out here to get money. Fuck em and suck em when you need to, but that's it. It's not about love in this game. The game is a business."

That was the first and last time Reina ever touched me like that.

4 RO

Now, don't get me wrong, just because I wasn't interested in the high school boys does not mean I didn't fuck em and let em eat my pussy from time to time. Especially Ro.

He was my first, the first guy who ever penetrated me. I had been fingered by other guys, but never fully fucked until I met Ro. I never told him that he was my first.

I like to think of him as my high school sweetheart, if I had such a thing.

He was tall, about 6'2 with smooth dark skin. His skin was free of any blemishes and it was not apparent that he was a kid from his facial hair. He wore a very clean beard that met the side of his face.

He had a slender build with broad shoulders, the body of a god. You could definitely tell that he didn't waste any time in the gym. He was, after all, the football star.

Ro was Reina's age.

One thing I loved about Ro was the way he smelled. He had a fresh smell of cologne all the time, the kind that makes your panties wet. His skin was so smooth, people was always mistaking the nigga for a Dominican or some shit.

I remember the first day I saw him. Me and Reina decided to blow something and hit the football game. We wasn't on shit, decided it was going to be a laid back kind of day.

As I'm chilling watching the game, I see this nigga go down, hard. Ro had slammed into him so hard that the nigga lost his balance. Then the coach called Ro off the field.

As he angrily walked off the field I saw him take off his helmet. That nigga was fine and watching him sent tingles in my pussy.

I told Reina, "Bitch, I gotta have him, who is that?!" She said, "Oh, girl that's Ro, the cheerleaders' most wanted nigga in the high school, Summer, he ain't got no money of his own, don't waste your time."

Reina talked about all the girls Ro had had his way with and then passed them off to one of his friends.

"He really doesn't take much interest to the high school girls, especially not those needy ass cheerleaders. His family is wealthy so he's used to bitchs throwing themselves at him.

Don't waste your time SUMMER!" Her words sounded in my ears as if they were filled with water. My pussy had overtaken the desire for logic. I wanted him.

I told Reina I'd catch up to her and I waited around as the field emptied out. It felt like I waited for that nigga for an hour before he finally walked out of the team's locker room.

He came out with a group of his friends, but I wasn't shy about it. I walked right up to him and said, "Aye shorty, I'm…"

"Summer, yea, I know. It's hard not to know who you are when you're that fine." He gave me a little grin and his friends, all grinning at me and looking at me like I was a piece of steak to a hungry pack of wolves, walked off ahead.

We chilled on the football field's benches and just chopped it up for what seemed like hours. We talked about everything from our parents to his plans for college.

Ro was an only trust fund child and his parents had very high expectations for him. He didn't drink or smoke. He worked out regularly, studied hard, and partied when he had the time. I told him that I didn't think college was for me and he didn't seem like he judged me. He gave me a "you never know" shrug and moved on in the conversation.

At about 11 it must have dawned on him that it had gotten late. The game had ended at eight o'clock and we were still talking. It wasn't anything left on but one street light shining on the field, he turned to me and said, "Summer, can I offer you a ride home?"

"Yea, that's cool". We started walking to the parking lot and he grabbed my hand. That shit started sending all kinds of sparks through my pussy and I knew that I was going to fuck him that night. I had on a short pleated skirt so all he would have had to do was slide it up, move my panties to the side, and stick his dick in. The wind blowing on my pussy didn't make it any better either. I wanted to speed up the process but one thing I could never seem like and that was thirsty for a nigga. So I just chilled as we walked to his whip.

We got to his car. Much to my surprise, he was not driving what I always imagined a high school boy would drive. He drove a royal blue BMW 350 with black leather seats. When he opened the door for me there were blue lights on the passenger side and driver's side that lit up the dashboard and the floor. His radio looked like a small television and had a multifunction navigation system. The car smelled like he had just taken it from the lot an hour ago. It wasn't even a crumb on the floor.

"Summer, where you stay?" Ro asked. I stay close, I'll tell you when to turn, just pull out of here and turn left."

When he started the call up the muthafucka chimed, "Hello Roosevelt, welcome back, what is your destination?' Ro responded, "Hello Cecilia, I will be manually navigating this trip" and the car started up.

His shit was so dope. I said, "Damn, how you afford something like this?" He told me it was a gift from his parents. I had to check to make sure my mouth wasn't opened. How the hell did this nigga have more than one parent and how the hell could they afford a car like this for their teenage kid? That shit was crazy. Here I am with a coked out prostitute as a mama who ain't never gave me shit more than some clothes and fucking lessons and this nigga got a BMW! There was a part of me that envied him and it became very prevalent. The ride to my house was pretty much silent.

When we pulled up to my house Ro reached for his door handle to get out. "Naw, don't get out. This ain't the type of neighborhood you trust with this type of car."

He opened the door as if he didn't even hear what the fuck I said. He walked around the car and opened my car door for me to get out.

"Ro, you ain't gotta walk me to my door or no shit like that. Gone get in your whip and go home. I wanna make sure Mommy and Daddy get their Prince home safely."

Again, as if he didn't hear what the fuck I said, he grabbed my hand and walked me to my raggedy ass apartment door. When we got to my apartment door he turned to me and said, "Summer, I'd love to take you out some time."

"Yea, maybe. I'll see you around." I leaned in to kiss him but he kissed me on my cheek and turned to walk back out the apartment. What the fuck?! It was clear that I wasn't going to be able to fuck this nigga that night so I opened up the door and went in the crib.

When I got in the crib Mama was gone as usual. I looked in the fridge, for what reason I don't know. As expected, it was a half-gallon of spoiled ass milk, some of the half eaten restaurant food from earlier in the week, and that goddamn baking soda. I hated that baking soda so much. Seeing the shit made me sick. I slammed the fridge door shut, went into the front room and slammed down on my air mattress. I closed my eyes to relax and all I could smell was Ro's cologne. My pussy did what it does best, it began to tingle.

That day I had gone to school looking like a naughty school girl. I had on a white Chanel collar shirt that had mid sleeves with the button open just enough to see the area between my titties and my Victoria Secret lace black bra. I was rocking it with a Chanel cheerleader type skirt with plaid print and I had on thigh high socks and Gucci loafers. Niggas loved my hair and bitches envied it so I wore my hair down, which was long, black and straight, with just a tad of wave to it.

As I was lying on the air mattress thinking about this nigga and how fine he was I started running my hands softly down my titties. That shit felt so good so I unbuttoned my shirt, but I did it slowly as if he was there watching me, just the way Mama taught me and I let it open. I could feel the air on my bare belly and it made my nipples hard.

I was even more aroused. I pulled my bra up and started to play with my nipples. A moan slipped my lips and I moved my hand to my belly. As I moved my hand down from my belly I could feel the soft fabric of the skirt on the skin of my legs. The breeze coming in from the window caused the skirt to move. I moved my fingers underneath my skirt and into the top of my black lace Victoria Secret panties.

That's where they met my pussy and I began to finger myself so softly. I moaned. I wanted more. I took my fingers out of my pussy and licked them. Then I sucked them.

I put them back in my pussy and I moved them in and out back and forth. I played with my clit and rubbed the sides. The moans, they slipped from my lips louder and louder. I began to shove my fingers in my pussy harder and harder.

My pussy let off juices and I could hear the squish as I shoved them into my pussy. It turned me on more. I took my other hand and I grabbed my nipple on my titty and I pulled it and throttled it.

Back and forth in my pussy, harder. I was moving my ass to the flow of my pussy. The tingle was loud and aggressive now.
"Ooohhh...yeesss...Fuccckkk..." I screamed.

And that's when I felt it, this is what she wanted, that feeling. I started to shake but I didn't stop shoving my fingers into my pussy. "Fucccckkkkkkkk". I was wet. I didn't get up to clean myself up, I didn't cover myself up; I just rolled over and went to sleep.

The next day at school Reina told me that she knew that I had stayed to wait for Ro. I didn't deny it and she wasn't happy about it at all.

I knew I liked him, but I knew that there would never be an "us". He was a high school boy and he wasn't in my league. Reina would make sure of that anyway. She demanded me to be focused at all times.

I saw Ro from time to time in the hallways. Some days he would come sit down at the lunch table and chop it up with me and Reina. Reina was reserved with Ro, but not nasty. She would mainly just listen as he and I talked amongst ourselves and eat her lunch barely looking up.

I always shot down his "take me out" requests. He became a regular at buying me gifts that he could afford on a high school kid's salary I guess, and waiting for me after school. I didn't understand why he didn't just use the money that he had readily access to. He worked a part time job as a camp instructor for kids. Ro always talked some bullshit about wanting to be independent of his parents. He just didn't know how good he had it.

I would fuck him and suck his dick whenever I felt like it. He would eat my pussy anywhere and on demand. It's what I loved about him most. He knew just how to make me feel good and he wasn't clingy like the other niggas I was fucking and sucking.

I usually would have him take me home, park in the back, and let my seat back. He'd eat it until I came in his mouth and I'd get out and go in the house. I never let him come in that shit hole and he didn't pressure me. We would fuck on the benches of the football field after his games and the field emptied. I'd sit on him and ride him while he sucked my titties so softly. Sometimes I'd kiss him, but not often. I didn't want him to become attached.

I'd usually fuck him if I saw him out with another bitch. I remember I saw him at the pizza joint later in the year and he was with this one chic. She was pretty, a mixed girl with blue eyes, curly shoulder length brown hair, slender build with a small waist, small titties that sat upright and didn't require a bra, and a perfectly shaped ass; but she definitely wasn't fucking in my business.

 I walked in the restaurant and walked past their table. I walked into the back. I never even had to say a word or look at him. Ro excused himself for a moment to go to the bathroom. He followed me into the Women's bathroom. We never said a word to each other. I hopped up on the sink inside the single person bathroom of the pizza joint, lifted my already short ass dress, leaned back and he ate my pussy. I came all over his mouth and he continued to eat it until I was finished climaxing. When he finished eating it, he pulled down his pants and he fucked me until he came. He nibbled at my nipple and licked my neck while grabbing my ass and I moaned.

Fuck me muthafucka, I'm in control." He fucked me harder and when I felt him about to nut and I pushed him off me. I hopped down turned to lean over the sink and he ate my pussy from the back and then he ate my ass. I busted in his mouth again, feeling the pussy juices streaming down my leg.

He grabbed my waist and he fucked me hard and I squealed from pain and excitement. I came again. He became even more aroused. He moaned, and then he clenched me hard enough to bruise my waist and I felt him fill me up like a lake. He laid still for a moment, then he pulled out of me.

I cleaned up and left him to enjoy the rest of his date. Fucking, that's what we did. But that was it. It was never going to go anywhere else.

5 EIGHTEEN

High school was easy. I was smart so I didn't struggle and Reina wasn't into school so she did the bare minimum to pass. She finished before me so she would usually just hit me when I got out to meet up. She had already had her own crib since the day I met her, but she was always really private about her living arrangements. I just assumed she was in a fucked up situation like me. I didn't press her to ever meet at her house, or know where she lived. I figured, she would tell me when she was ready.

When I graduated Reina was the only one that showed up for me. It didn't matter. I was used to Mama being gone on binges and I was eighteen now. I had been in the game long enough to know how to take care of myself. I only attended the graduation to keep the counselors off my back and out of my business. I didn't need any of them nosey ass honkeys in my business, worried about my living situation. So I went. It was just business.

"Summer, why don't you get your shit and come stay with me?" Reina asked me one day a few days after I graduated. I was stunned. I mean, after all, I didn't even know where Reina lived. She had plenty of niggas so I knew she didn't need to work. Was that how she took care of herself?

She drove a black Mercedes Benz CL 550 with the chrome wheels on it. It had chocolate leather seats in it and you could hear her coming from 10 blocks away. She always wore Gucci for the most part which wasn't shocking to me because I pretty much did too. Sometimes I'd wear Chanel, and we both wore Giuseppe Zanotti often.

From the looks of it her niggas gave her more money than mine did. I still didn't have a car but I had expensive clothing and handbags. I always kept my hair did and one of my niggas made me a standing appointment at the salon weekly. He liked my hair long, black, straight, and the way it laid in the middle of my back.

My niggas treated me to the finest gifts so I kept a stock of Tiffany jewelry that I usually hid. I didn't know if Mama would take it.

She loved my shit and she would fancy herself with my gifts. I don't know why because she had plenty of shit from her Johns. She could start her own Tiffany Collection store if she could stay off the coke long enough.

I knew Mama would never touch the clothes, it was important to her that I kept up my appearance, that would be the only way I'd find a dope boy and keep him. I had to look the part.

Mama always kept my clothes on hangers in the bedroom closet and sometimes when I needed to get dressed, I'd come in while she was fucking her John in my panties and bra to pick out my clothing.

The Johns would practically be drooling and Mama would smile at me. "That's Summer, she's gorgeous isn't she? Now you're going to have to pay extra for peeping at my Summer."

Anything that I had with no real value was a gift from Ro. I kept the gifts as a keepsake in case he ever asked me about them. I didn't want him to see me as I really was.

Sometimes I wore some of it to school. I knew how important it was to him. He would always "light up" when he saw something he had bought. That shit was few and far between though.

I was on a mission. It didn't really fit with my appearance and Reina wasn't very happy when I did it.

I don't know why he didn't buy me more expensive gifts, his family was loaded. I'm sure he could have easily stolen money from his parents or even just asked for it.

I had three Rolexes. My favorite one from one of my niggas was a Rollie with diamonds around the face of it. The band was real gold and it was worth ten thousand dollars. I wore that Rolex the most.

"You can't keep living there trying to look after your mama. One day she ain't gonna come home Summer". Her words stung me like a bee and I felt tears welling up in my eyes.

"Look, this coke shit is real and it has yo mama. Crying about it ain't gone do shit. It took my mama and I had to deal with it. I'm trying to save you the trouble. You practically take care of yourself anyway. Yo Mama wanted you to have a better life than her, that's what she was trying to teach you in her own way. You ain't gone have that life living in no shit hole."

It was a harsh reality but it was one I had to come to terms with.

"Stop me by the crib so I can grab my shit" I told Reina.

6 TJ

We pulled up to the crib. As soon as we went in the house I saw Mama on my air mattress with one of her Johns. They were both butt ass naked.

They didn't seem to hear that somebody else came in the house because neither of them bothered to wake up. On the kitchen table there was an envelope addressed to mama, the aluminum foil, white power, and a razor.

I didn't know that people could get coke in the mail, but I guess times was changing. Someone had clearly mailed Mama a care package. It was evident that she and the John had indulged in it.

Reina didn't seemed bothered at the sight of the coke left in the open. I grabbed a pen and a piece of paper from the kitchen drawer and wrote Mama a quick note.

"I won't be here when you wake up. I'll come back for you when I can. Protect yourself. Be safe -Summer".

I quickly started packing up my things and Reina and I hauled bags down to her car. It seemed to take forever and there was so much shit that I could not fit in the car.

On the about the third trip back to the apartment there was a knock on the door. Who the hell was knocking on our door? We never had visitors unless it was a John and they never just showed up. It was a rule of Mama's that her Johns never come over unaccompanied by her and they had respected that rule for as long as I existed.

Reina looked at me and I shrugged my shoulders. As she was walking to the door she lifted the back of her shirt and pulled out a twenty two caliber gun with a pearl pink handle.

Where the fuck did Reina get a gun from and why didn't I know she had it? Had she always been carrying a gun?

This was no time for those types of questions when an uninvited guest was at the door.

"Who the fuck is it?" Reina shouted. There was no answer. The door sounded with a knock again and Reina pointed the pistol while opening the door. The pistol met the nose of the most gorgeous nigga I had ever laid eyes on.

He was even more gorgeous than Ro. This nigga was a god.

He was as dark as midnight, about six feet two inches tall with a medium build, deep dimples, a gold grill, low haircut that displayed a deep wave pattern, and broad shoulders. You could see his muscles budging from his collar shirt.

He looked to be in his early 30s at most. He was dressed like he was going to work with a white collar button up, tan slacks that displayed his dick print, and a pair of white Salvatore Ferragamos and a tan and white belt to match. I could smell the Tom Ford cologne that he was wearing from the door. I would have fucked him right there if Reina wasn't distracting me.

Was he one of Mama's Johns? All sort of questions ran through my head. If he was a John this would definitely be one that we would fuck together.

"Damn baby, you gone invite me here to shoot me?" the visitor asked while snickering, clearly unaffected by the fact that a bitch had a pistol to his face.

"I didn't invite your muthafuckin ass here and what the fuck do you want?!" Reina asked in the coldest voice I had ever heard her speak in.

"I'm TJ and I'm looking for Maddy, she asked me to deliver a package for her. But I can see Maddy is a little preoccupied so I can come back."

I was instantly embarrassed. I was so distracted with the knock that I didn't cover Mama up.

I quickly walked to the door, "No, what package? I'm Summer, Maddy's daughter.

I know you didn't come all the way over here just to bring mail so what is it?"

"Summer", he repeated with a smile and handed me the package. "Tell yo Mama I billed it to her credit account."

My pussy was instantly excited. The smell of his cologne and his sensual smile made me want him. Reina never took the pistol down. There she stood next to me, me wanting him, and her pointing her pistol without even a flinch.

"Summer, you're all grown up now. You call me if you need anything" and he handed me a business card as he turned and walked away. All grown up? Had we met before? I definitely would have remembered meeting a god and so would my pussy. How did he know me?

Reina didn't give me time to ask any questions. She quickly closed the door. I sat the coke on the table with the rest of the white powder, stuck his business card in my Chanel purse, peeked out the window to see him hop in his silver Cadillac Escalade, and we continued packing the rest of the shit that I was going to take.

As we were taking the last bag that could fit in Reina's car down I could tell something was on her mind. When something was bothering Reina she always got quiet and seemed distant.

"What's up Rei? What's on your mind?" I asked her, hoping this wouldn't be one of them times she shut me out. She was very private so there were many times where she wouldn't tell me shit, ignoring my questions as if I never asked them.

"Summer, I don't like that nigga. I saw the excitement in your eyes when you looked at him, but something about him doesn't sit well with me. I know you ain't gone listen to me because you never do, but you be careful with him."

Reina was right, I wasn't going to take heed to her warnings. I didn't give a shit what kind of feeling she had about him. I had a feeling about him too and I wanted him. I wanted to feel him inside of me. I wanted to know what his tongue felt like. I wanted him and that is exactly what I was going to get.

We got in Reina's whip and pulled out of the neighborhood. Reina was talking but I couldn't understand what she was saying. My head was clouded with thoughts about TJ and what he would do to me.

"Summer, Summer, SUMMER!" Reina yelled. "What's up Rei? My fault, what were you saying?" I asked her.

"Summer, you are about to enter a very restricted area with me. It's not an area that I've ever let anyone into and I want to make sure you're ready because once you are in, there is no getting out" Reina said in a very stern voice.

"Reina, you're my best friend. If you're in it, I'm in it, always and forever."

"Always and forever" Reina repeated with me and I grabbed her hand from the armrest where it was resting. Reina looked at me and smiled.

7 THE NEXT CHAPTER

We drove for what seemed like forever. I had never been out of the hood so I didn't really have the concept of what direction we were heading. I could definitely tell that the looks of the neighborhoods started changing the longer we drove.

It was the cleanest I had ever seen the world look. The neighborhoods had grass without missing patches and palm trees. The lawns were all neatly manicured and the cars were not parked on the street; instead they were parked in the large driveways in front of their garages that looked like houses of their own.

About an hour later we made a turn and met a gate with a security guard and slowly pulled up to it.

"Miss Reina, hello, I hope that your trip went well. I see you have a guest" the guard said after approaching Reina's window.

"Hello Ramone" Reina said in an unfamiliar voice, "Actually, this is Summer, she will be staying with me for some time. I'd like for you to make sure she doesn't have issues getting in when she comes and goes if she is without me."

"Of course, Miss Reina, I'll make sure the other shifts are aware, have a good night" Ramone said as he opened the gate for us to drive in.

As we drove into the gate I was expecting to pull up to a house; instead the gate opened into a neighborhood that had houses big as fuck that stretched over acres of land. The neighbors were not really neighbors because you couldn't even walk to the house next door. You need a car or a fancy ass go cart.

Reina drove through the neighborhood quietly and then we pulled into a driveway. Reina shut the car down and motioned for me to get out. I got out the car and stood looking quietly at the house. There was no way in the fuck this girl could afford to pay for a house of this magnitude. There had to be someone else living there, maybe she was living with her father.

Just then, a guy came out dressed in a tuxedo. "Luis, please unload Miss Summer's bags from the car and place her things in the wing where she'll be staying. Reina grabbed my hand and dragged (Brown, 2018)me in the house.

When Reina opened the door to the house I thought I was looking at some television shit. The marble floors and the fancy chandeliers left me speechless. There was a stairwell that spiraled to the top of the staircase where a Mexican lady in a maid's uniform stood dusting the banister. I followed Reina through the house like a zombie, hoping to get a glimpse of the people that she lived with.

Reina led me up the spiral staircase and past the Mexican lady with the maid's outfit on. As we walked down the long hallway, I could see several rooms that we were decorated. Some were bedrooms, there were two sitting rooms, a library, what looked like a winery, a white room, a room full of paintings, and a workout room.

When we reached the end of the hall Reina opened a set of double doors and ushered me in. "Summer, this is where you will be sleeping" Reina said, as she led me into a huge vintage room.

The room had a King size bed with expensive linen on it and was neatly made. There was a pearl white vintage Florencia Carved loveseat with the matching chair positioned neatly in the corner. Between the two was a Victoria console table with an antique tea set.

In the opposite corner of the room was an antique mirror stand that sat outside a dress form and crystal sculpture of a naked woman. Reina led me threw the room to the room's master bath that included a toilet that washed your ass after you flush, a hot tub with a separate shower, and a double sink that had a vanity mirror with the matching chair built between it.

This room and bathroom could have been three of the apartment that I lived in with Mama. I had never even seen a room like this in anything other than television shows. This was insane.

Reina showed me the closet where I'd be storing my clothes. When she opened the double doors to the walk in closet it was full. It was clothes on every hanger. There was Gucci, Chanel, Dolce & Gabbana, Louis Vuitton, Yves St Laurent, and some designer shit I had never even heard of. I didn't know where she expected my shit to fit.

She walked into the closet and I followed behind her and we walked back until we approached a turn where the wall was standing. The turn opened into another closet that had only designer shoes on shelves and purses on the opposite shelves.

As if Reina could read my mind, she said, "Summer, all of these things belong to you. You can choose to keep the stuff you brought with you or get rid of it. It's up to you. Let me know if you need more space and I'll have Maria show you to your storage space."

Ok, this shit was too weird and I could barely take it anymore. "Reina, where are the people that lives here with you?" I asked.

Reina chuckled at me, "I'm looking at her" she said. I could not believe that Reina owned this all by herself. I knew one thing, I wanted this life for myself.

"Where are my manners?" Reina asked. She walked over to the nightstand by the bed and picked up the phone. "Luis, please bring our guest a snack" and she hung up the phone. "Summer, get unpacked and get comfortable. I'll be back to check on you later" she said as she walking out of the room.

She turned toward me before she closed the door, "We dine at seven o'clock and we're having guests so please dress accordingly." Reina disappeared behind the door.

8 A SNACK BEFORE DINNER

I was overwhelmed and exhausted from the moving. It was already five o'clock and I wanted to take a nap so I slipped out of my clothes and ran my bath water. After getting into the bath, I soaked for about 30 minutes, washed myself and got out. As I was looking for something comfortable to slip on, there was a knock on the door.

"Yes?" I asked. "Miss Summer" a voice said that sounded like English was the second language, "Miss Reina requested that I bring you a snack" the voice responded. "Oh, ok, perfect, I'm starving" I said and darted to the door to open it.

When I opened the door there was the butler that I met earlier, Luis, and another gentleman with a leash around his neck. Luis quickly handed me the leash to the man and disappeared down the hallway. What in the entire fuck was this?!

The man was absolutely gorgeous. He a Latino, about six feet three inches tall with a muscular build. He had a short haircut but you could clearly tell that the texture of his hair was originally curly. He had a perfect tan and smelled of a cologne that was familiar but unknown. He was dressed in a pair of underwear that showed his very large dick print and nothing else. He didn't even have on shoes. I didn't know what to do so I pulled him in by the leash and shut the door.

When I shut the door we stood eye to eye looking at one another. He didn't even smile. "What is it that I'm supposed to do with you?' I asked. He didn't respond. "Hello, do you talk?!" I screamed in his face.

He got down on one knee and bowed to me. Still, he said nothing. "I order you to speak to me" I said, trying it to see if it would work.

He responded, "I have only one order, to please you. I do not speak unless I am given permission. I do not make any moves without being told while you hold the leash" he finished.

I quickly removed the leash expecting to talk to him about what was happening. As soon as I unsnapped the leash from his neck band, he picked me up and carried me to the bed.

He pulled opened my robe and began to suck my titty. His tongue was so soft and I moaned as he rubbed his hand down my belly in between my legs where his fingers met my pussy.

He inserted his two fingers into my pussy, but he did it slowly. By now my pussy was wet and I craved him. He kissed my neck while fingering me. The kisses went down my neck, back to each of my titties, then over my belly button.

I felt him take his thumb and place it in my ass hole and push it gently just before his tongue took over my clit. He kissed my pussy like he was making love to it and he licked it while fingering me in my pussy and ass at the same time. I grabbed his head and wrapped my legs around his head. He didn't gasp for air or stop. He seemed unbothered by my grasp.

I moaned and I pushed my body down so that his fingers would go further inside of me. My body warmed up and then I felt a glory. My pussy tingled like it had never tingled before and I squealed in excitement. The feeling held, not like any other time before where it was quick and over. It held, the feeling of my pussy and I hollered. "OOOHHHHHHMMYYYYYGOOOODDDDDDD" and I left off an explosion of nut that splashed over his face in dept.

He pulled up, cum leaking from his mouth and cheek area, rubbed his dick against my wet pussy. I moaned and grabbed him. I wanted him to stick it in. I wanted to feel him.

He flipped me over and put me on all fours. Cool, I thought, this nigga is about to tear it up from the back. Just then he inserted his dick into my ass. I cried out in pain and tried to move up to get him out so that the anguish would stop, but he held me and started to fuck me in my ass. I was fighting to get him off of me. I screamed, "Stop, please, you're hurting me!"

He grabbed my waist hard and jammed his dick into my ass, then he took his other hand and stuck four of his fingers into my pussy. I was about to scream, but the pleasure took over me. The pain stopped. I groaned in pleasure and I began to slob on the bedspread.

'Ohhhhh, what the fuuuccckkk?!!! I wannnttt you so bad, don't stop" I begged. He continued to fuck me slowly and the pleasure was so intense I felt like I would pass out in pleasure. All of a sudden I felt a pleasure that I'd never experienced before and like a whirlpool my pussy whooshed out with cum all over the covers and all down my legs. He pulled his fingers from my pussy and his dick from my ass, removed himself from the bed and bowed on one knee.

I rolled over on the bed in my own cum out of exhaustion. "You are dismissed" I said. He responded, "Please leash me and call my Master to send for me." I quickly got off of the bed, picked up the leash and connected it to his neck band.

I took the leash to walk around the bed to the night stand that held the phone and he crawled behind me. I picked up the phone ready to dial Reina's cell phone number, but instead there was a familiar voice.

"Miss Summer, have you completed your snack?" Luis asked. "Yes" I whispered with what little energy I had left.

"Please hook the leash on the outside of your room door and someone will collect your tray" and he hung up the phone.

I walked the snack over to the door and opened the door naked, still dripping of cum. He wore nothing but his leash. I led him outside of the door and hooked the leash to the door knob, closed the door, and got on the bed where it was clean and dry. Just as I was about to close my eyes and drift off to sleep, the phone on the night stand rang.

I answered, "Hello?" "Summer, get dressed, it's already six thirty" Reina said. "Rei, can I skip dinner? I'm exhausted from my snack" I replied. "No, it's a business dinner. Get showered and dressed, see you in a half hour, Luis will show you down" Reina said before hanging up.

I mustered up what little energy I had left and got myself into the bathroom to run myself a shower. I stood under the water letting it hit my now sore body and wash away the significant amount of cum that I still had dripping from my pussy. This snack had took my body somewhere it had never been before but I know I wanted it to go back again. I finished washing clean and got out of the shower.

I went into the closet and looked through my new wardrobe before grabbing a black Alexander McQueen dress with the low cut and back out down from the hanger. I went to my back and grabbed my favorite pair of Jimmy Choo strappy heels and my Victoria Secret bra and panty set that had the matching garner.

After I was dressed I set at the vanity set to give myself a smoky eye and a red lip. Then I squirted some Gucci Guilty from my bag on my cleavage and between my legs. By the time I was ready it was six fifty. Just then I heard a knock on the door. "Miss Summer, may I show you to dinner?" Luis said.

I opened the bedroom door and he escorted me down the long hall, through the double doors, down the stairwell, past the front door, and to the dining hall that had a long table with Reina seated at the head and some mysterious men seated on both sides of the table. There was ten chairs on both sides, one chair at the head, and the other chair at the end of the table.

When I walked in the men all gasp in excitement and disbelief. They were all dressed in suit and ties with clean shaves and were all standing behind their chairs.

Reina motioned for me to be seated and Luis pulled out the chair at the long opposite end from Reina. I sat down and smiled at Reina.

Reina nodded and all the men took a seat. When they were seated a wait staff that contained more people than I seen when I came in the house brought out food and set the table. They placed all of the food on our plates and filled our glasses with a bottle that read Italian red wine from Italy.

After the food was placed on the plates, no one picked up a fork to eat, so I followed suit. Then Reina picked up her fork to eat, ate a couple bites, nodded and everyone else picked up their food to eat. The table was completely silent other than the sounds of the forks hitting the plates.

I had been Reina's best friend since freshman year of high school; and I had spent every day with her. But, it was evident that I knew nothing about her at all.

Reina was always a girl that was rough around the edges with it all together to me, but that's it; she was a girl. Now I saw someone, something, different. Suddenly, I was afraid of her.

9 BUSINESS NEGOTIATIONS

As if on cue, when Reina finished her meal, the table was cleared by the wait staff. It didn't seem to matter that some were still eating. Their plates and glasses were removed from in front of them. Once the table was cleared the wait staff disappeared into the other room.

"Gentlemen, meet Miss Summer, my new business partner", Reina said in a stern tone. "I expect that she will be provided with the same respect given to me, let's get down to business. Luis?"

Suddenly Luis appeared. "Yes, Miss Reina?" he asked. "Provide an overview of the parlor's business."

Luis started in his heavy accented English, "Today the Table did five hundred thousand dollars for the dinner course. We sold two dinner entrees which are running at two hundred and fifty thousand dollars apiece, market rate. We sold twelve snacks at eight thousand three hundred and thirty three dollars, a combination of white chocolate and dark chocolate. Profit was just under one hundred thousand dollars. We sold three desserts for thirty two thousand dollars apiece, a ninety six thousand dollar profit.

"For the real estate we have twelve operational houses that hold twelve keys to each. The walls are pure white and we seem to be at the top of the market. Two keys are delivered to new owners every hour. Profit for last week was over a million dollars."

"We have also recently acquired a new clinic as well where we employ two new Pharmacists. The previous clinics that employed the Pharmacists were closed down due to violations permanently. "

"There also appears to be an issue with one of the patients at one of the clinics. He has declined the offer to become a home owner", Luis concluded. Luis walked over to Reina and handed her a card. "This was left by the difficult patient, he wanted to have it passed along in case "whomever was in charge" decided to talk."

35

Reina took the card from Luis and placed it underneath the placemat on the table. "We'll handle this later", she told Luis.

One of the gentlemen from the table stood up. "We are expanding the Table to include a roundtable where customers can converse with others while enjoying the snack option. So far it has been a success and the demand for reservations has increased, permission to raise the prices."

"What is the reservation price currently?" Reina asked. "Fifteen thousand dollars per guest or two for twenty five thousand dollars. The Governor would like a discounted rate for a regular standing reservation. Currently the roundtable can seat ten customers" he responded.

Reina thought about what the gentleman had said for a moment. "No, the price stands. The Governor cannot have a discounted rate unless she provides something beneficial for the business. How far are we booked for this special?" Reina asked.

"Two months out", the gentleman responded. Reina nodded and he took a seat.

"Luis, bring out Miss Summer's snack please." Luis disappeared behind the door to the kitchen area and came back shortly with the man on the leash.

He was cleaned up as if he had never fucked the life out of me, but stood there in a different pair of underwear and a different color leash. He did not look my way at all, but instead looked at the floor without blinking. Luis tugged him a bit and walked him over to Reina. He bowed down on his knees and kissed her had that laid on the chair. She seemed unaffected by the sign of affection from the man.

"Summer, did you enjoy this snack?" Reina asked looking at me with a straight, but stern face. "I did" I replied in a serious tone.

Reina scooted back from the long table carefully, far enough for everyone to have a full view of her entire body. As she scooted the man began to crawl around on the leash back and forth as if he was a dog about to play with the owner. Luis wrapped the leash around his hand to regain control.

Reina looked gorgeous and grown up, even in her serious place. She was dressed in a short red lace Gucci dress with no bra and a full view of her perfect titties and black Christian Louboutins. She had her hair pulled back into a very neat long ponytail and had a black lip accompanied by a smoky eye.

After she pulled back from the table she slumped in her chair a bit and opened her leg. Luis unsnapped the leash on the man and he quickly crawled over to Reina's chair.

He crawled up to Reina; she looked at him and rubbed his head. He looked up at her for approval and she nodded. The man went between her legs and began to lick rapidly. Reina didn't look at the rest of us sitting in the room and the men at the table did not seem uncomfortable by the fact that the boss was getting her pussy ate at the dinner table.

Reina moaned in enjoyment and the man grabbed her legs and wrapped them around his neck. She grabbed his head and held it between her legs. Luis disappeared behind the door for a moment and returned with a covered dish. He stood by watching Reina as she enjoyed her pleasure.

Then Reina yelled out in excitement and I could see her legs shake from my chair. She took her legs from around the man's leg and he crawled away. Luis passed the dish to one of the gentlemen seated at the table. He stood up, went over and opened the dish.

Reina sat there with her head leaned back on the chair with a slight look of exhaustion. He sat the dish on the table and took the towel from it, wrung it out, and began to wipe Reina's pussy clean. Reina slid down as he wiped the areas surrounding her pussy and ass. Once he was finished he placed the towel back in the dish, covered it, and Luis picked the dish up and disappeared behind the door again.

Reina scooted back to the table and Luis walked over to reapply the leash to the man. He walked the man out of the dining room.

"This snack is more than good, would you agree Summer?" Reina asked. "Yes, I do", I replied. "Put him on the special course at the roundtable, she told the gentleman at the table. He's going to be in high demand."

"Yes ma'am", the man responded. Reina looked at one of the other gentleman seated at the table, "And the patient that's being difficult, get it handled" she said.

Reina waived her hand and all the men from both sides got up from the table and filed out of the door exiting the dining room.

As soon as the room was empty Reina got up from her chair and walked down toward me. She took a seat in the chair next to mine. "Summer, I'm sure you have many questions and soon you'll get the answers" Reina sighed.

"Reina", I interrupted. "I'm not sure what I want to ask first. I'm not sure if I understand the snack that you sent to the room, or the dinner we just had. But more importantly, I'm not sure I know who you are. We've been best friends since my freshman year in high school and I'm learning that I know nothing about you at all. I'm sure I can manage to find my way to my sleeping quarters" I said as I stood up to walk out.

Reina was quiet as I exited the dining room and Luis soon found me in the hall to escort me to my room. We both walked in silence and I thanked him when I reached my bedroom door.

When I walked in the room I could see the linen had been changed. The room smelled fresh and all of my things were put away.

I laid across the bed and let the thoughts run through my head. Everything was like a puzzle to me and I wanted to try to put it together on my own. After all, it's not like I could trust Reina to tell me when I wanted her to.

So Reina runs a business that sells men, or maybe their services; that must be what the dinner talk was about at the table. But what was the real estate? Where was the parlor? And the clinic, was she talking about dope? Who were all of the men at the table? Obviously, they must work for her. And whose card did Luis pass Reina? Who was the problem that needed to be handled?" I wondered as I dosed off to sleep.

10 CLASS

The dreams that I had that night were none of my usual dreams. Reina, my best friend, was a monster in my dreams and she did horrible things. I tossed and turned all night. At about 2:00 am I woke up in a cold sweat.

I laid in the bed looking at the ceiling for what seemed like forever, thinking, how had I been Reina's friend for so long and known nothing about her? How had Reina hid this lifestyle from me? Is that someone that could really be trusted? I had given Reina full access to my life. She knew about Mama, seen my living conditions, and she was the first person to ever teach me how to master the sensation of pleasure to my pussy without attachment. I was restless so I decided to take a walk through the house in hopes of tiring myself out.

I got up, took off my dress that I had obviously fell asleep in, exposing my panties and bra, slipped on my robe and crept out my bedroom. I tried my best to do it as quietly as possible, as I didn't want Luis popping up anywhere. He somehow had been doing that since I'd been in the house.

I scrolled along the halls bare feet looking at the beauty of the house. The house was immaculate and it was spick and span. I ran my fingers along the expensive paintings on the wall until I reached the end of the hall.

I was about to walk down the stairs, but then I saw a door that looked identical to the door that opened to the wing of the house where I was staying. I couldn't help but feed my curiosity so I walked over to the door. I pressed my ear to the door to ensure that there were no sounds and I would not walk into a secret meeting that might cause Reina to kill me or something. I mean, who knows, the bitch is clearly crazy. With my ear pressed against the door I could hear voices, and they both sounded familiar.

"Rei, why did you bring her here?!" the familiar voice yelled.

"Why the fuck do you even care?" Reina asked in a very agitated tone. "You either fucking love me or you love fucking me. Either way, I'm good with that" she spat out.

"Baby, I love you. I just don't want anything fucking up your business" the familiar voice responded, in a now reassuring tone. "Shit could go very bad if we don't go about this the right way."

Reina must have been walking away because the voice said, "Rei, don't walk away from me. Come here. I'm sorry, I didn't mean to upset you."

I was trying my best to make out the voice, to figure out why it was so familiar to me. Who was in there with Reina and were they talking about me? But more importantly, Reina had a boyfriend, that she loved, and had never mentioned him. This bitch was just full of surprises.

Then the sounds of kissing started and you would think that I would have moved on, but I didn't. I sat there listening. I could hear Reina's moans and then I heard it. There was a sound that I knew. But no, it couldn't be. It was late so I clearly was starting to hallucinate.

I turned away from the door and walked quickly back toward my room. My mind and heart was racing. My breathing was happening quicker than I could control. By the time I got to my room door I was dizzy and I could not catch my breath. I reached over to turn the door knob to my room with the little strength I had left. Just as I stepped into my room and closed the door behind me, I collapsed onto the floor.

"Miss Summer, Miss Summer, are you alright?' Luis asked in his thick accent. "Why are you on the floor?" Luis continued, as he was helping to lift me onto the bed.

"I'm fine. I guess I was just really tired", I replied. He seemed satisfied with the answer and moved on to the next subject.

"Miss Summer, you need to get dressed. You have class in one hour" Luis said. "Oh, Luis, I'm not in school anymore. I'm eighteen. I graduated already" I informed him.

"Miss Reina requires that all employees attend classes. Get dressed, your uniform is hanging in the closet", he said in a matter of fact tone and disappeared outside of my bedroom door.

What kind of class was Reina *requiring* me to go to? I didn't move in to her house to be treated like a child and I didn't need this shit.

I got up to start packing my bags. I'd rather go back and live with Mama where I had independence and didn't have some type of pimp bitch running my future, than stay here and let her tell me what I could and couldn't do.

Suddenly, there was a knock on the bedroom door. *Great, could my day get any fucking worst, now I was probably going to have to have a confrontation with Reina. I'm sure she was not going to be pleased I was leaving.*

I walked over to the bedroom door and opened it. There stood a gorgeous nigga dressed in just his underwear and a collar for a leash, with a tray of food in hand.

"Your breakfast Madam", he said. I could not take my eyes off him and my pussy muscles began to throb. "Don't get distracted Summer", I said to myself. But, like a robot, my body moved itself out of the way of the door to allow him to come in.

He sat the tray of food on the bed stand and stood there, waiting for an order. I opened my robe and let it hit the floor.

"Come over here, now", I spat at him. He walked over to me and got on his knees awaiting further instructions. "What do you want?" I asked

"To please you Madam", he replied. I kicked him in the stomach.

"What do you want?!" I screamed. "To please you Madam" he replied again.

I kicked him in the stomach again, harder than before. "Stand the fuck up" I said as I kicked him again. He was now looking at me in my eyes, seeming pleasured by the fact that I was hurting him. "What the FUCK do you want muthafucka?!" I whispered in his face.

"To please you Madam", he replied in that same calm tone. I pushed him on to the bed so hard that his body did a slight bounce back up from the fall.

I pulled his underwear off. His dick was huge and it was hard as a rock as if the pleasure had already started. I took his dick into my mouth and I sucked it. I took it in and out and let it touch the back of my throat. I rubbed my hand in from the base of his dick to the tip while I sucked and the area became wet from my slob.

He groaned in intense pleasure and it made me excited to suck even more. I rubbed my fingers up to his nipples and I pulled just enough to give him a slight agony pleasure mixture. I moved my hand down to his balls and settled my knuckle in the area between his dick and balls and I sucked.

"Oh, no no no, stop, no no no", he said excitedly, attempting to remove his dick from my mouth. I wouldn't move. I mounted my legs on the bed and held fast continuing to suck. Then there was the taste of his warm salty cum filling in my mouth.

I continued to suck just enough to get all of the cum from his dick and then I swallowed and crawled up to sit on his face. I mounted over his mouth and he grabbed my legs to pull me down.

He licked me. His tongue was so warm and wet, the feeling drove my pussy wild; I could feel her begin to leak before we got all the way into it. "I will tell you when I'm ready to cum muthafucka", I scolded him.

He lifted my pussy from his mouth and tilted me forward and he ate my ass. I felt an intense erosion of an orgasm on its way and I screamed, "I WANT TO CUM NOW!" He quickly moved me back to have my pussy in his mouth and stuck his finger in my ass.

I squealed in excitement and I pushed down on his face and the feeling that I craved daily came and I erupted in cum all over his face. It was massive, like the first time Reina ate my pussy in the gym.

He didn't attempt to remove me from his face so I lifted to move myself off. As I did he grabbed me and scooted to the end of the bed. He carried me into the bathroom and sat me on the sink. I sat there not knowing exactly what was next.

He ran bath water for me and when it was finished he picked me up and put me in the bath. He washed my body until it was clean to satisfaction and extended his hand for me to step out and take the towel that he held for me.

When I stepped out of the bath tub and dried myself, he looked at me and said, "Is there anything else I can do for you before class Madam?"

"No, that will be all", I responded and he left.

I was having a good time, just maybe it wasn't so bad living with Reina. It was definitely worth a shot to see what the class was all about.

I grabbed a set of bra and panties from the drawer in the closet. I pulled the uniform off of the bathroom door where it had been left hanging for me. I dressed myself in the black corset, black blazer, and mini skirt, grabbed a pair of black strappy Jimmy Choos and raced toward the door.

When I opened the door Luis was waiting. "Miss Summer, follow me", he said. I walked quietly behind him as he led me down the long hallway to the stairwell.

We walked down the stairwell and he held my hand as if I was a princess.

Once we were down the stairwell we walked through the kitchen and there was another set of doors. When he opened the doors there was another long corridor. I started thinking that maybe I should have picked different shoes. Where the hell were we walking?

After about ten minutes, the corridor came to an end and there was a set of glass doors with the fog windows. Luis opened the door for me and motioned me in. As soon as I walked in I saw Reina seated at the desk. Alongside her were four of the men from the dinner table the other night.

Lesson 1

"Gentlemen, you met my business partner the other night, Summer", Reina said as she stood up to meet me. She pulled up out a chair on the same side of the desk as she was sitting on for me to sit down.

"Summer, I know you have a lot of questions right now and hopefully by the time we are done you will have them all answered. I am privileged to share my business with my best friend and trust that you will be an excellent leader."

"First order of business, understanding the business", Reina said. One of the gentlemen stood up as Reina sat down.

"Madam, my name is Black and I am the Governor for the East & West territories. I am responsible for all of the clinics and the employment of the pharmacists in those territories, as well as the real estate" he said as he pointed to a map on the desk. I also run the parlors there and employ the entrees, snacks, sides, and ala carts.

As I evaluated the territories, I could see that my old neighborhood was included. I didn't ask any questions. I sat quietly.

"Pardon me, let me ensure that you understand exactly what the lingo is for the business", he walked around the desk behind me and flicked a switch that looked like a light switch. A projector like screen rolled down and a PowerPoint started.

He explained the lingo for clinic was in relation to our Coke division. It was the only drug we operated in and the pharmacists- the actual employees who mixed and bagged the Coke lived on property around the clock. They were not allowed to leave and mostly worked in their underwear. Where the Coke was mixed and

43

cooked was called the Real Estate because the Pharmacists lived there with the key holder, or distro.

The territories, although governed by "Governors" always had a distro. These were the actual front line Supervisors, you could say, who made sure the real estate made the money it was supposed to, didn't skim, and had no problems. The Coke was always pure and we had the ingredients to mix shipped from El Salvador.

I met the other gentlemen who identified themselves as Blue, Silver, and Tan. The Governors never used names and were only identified by their aligned territory to their color.

Lesson 2

They explained the operation of the parlors or "tables" as they were called and the employees. There were different courses served at the tables and each table contained a different specialty course. The tables were specialty pleasure factories for high profile, rich women.

Women could come into the tables and choose their rooms. Some would come in for pussy eating pleasure, fingering pleasure, threesome pleasure, etc.

There were areas in the table where you could sit and talk with a guest while you were having your pussy eaten or even your toes licked. The courses did whatever you needed to be pleased and our menus were extensive and expensive.

Reservations were always required and exclusive; and we were always booked out. We served clients from the Governor of the city, FBI agents, crooked cops, and celebrities. You had to be in a certain financial bracket to receive an invitation.

The penalty for sharing an invite to the table, one of our clinics, or causing trouble to the organization was death. It was something that Reina did not waiver on. No one was excluded from the penalty should they break a rule of the organization, including me.

At that very moment I knew that I would never be able to just pack up and leave Reina's house. When she told me, in the car, that there was no turning back, she was serious. There was not a doubt in my mind that Reina would kill me without blinking. I was scared.

Lesson 3

The business was started by Reina's father who ran it successfully for years. He met Reina's mother at a Dominatrix clinic and fell in love with her. He was absolutely infatuated with her mother.

After they had Reina they groomed Reina at a young age. They didn't just groom her for the Coke business but they groomed her for the Parlor business too. Reina's father wanted her to take over the Parlor business.

Her parents sent Reina to train in a Dominatrix parlor when she turned ten years old. She watched them operate and the women there taught her about control. Reina learned to demand authority with her presence and how to sense her clients. She did well in her training and looked forward to taking over that area of their family business.

When Reina was fifteen, her father walked in on her mother having an affair with his business partner. He killed them both with a single shot to the head.

Reina was away at the Dominatrix parlor. When she returned home her father looked at her and said, "Reina, your mother broke the rules of the business and I had to put a bullet in her head".

Apparently, it was all business with her father after that. She was to take her mother's place and assume the Parlors, at fifteen years old. That is what she did. But, when she did that she somehow found out that her father was skimming money from the business and confronted him.

Her father supposedly disappeared and was never heard from again.

Reina broke down the profits from the businesses to me, the client list, and what a day to day operation looked like. She talked about competition and rules to handling competition that rejected our offers to join the organization. She pulled a 9MM from the desk drawer and slid it across the desk to me.

"Summer, this is yours. You are to NEVER be without it and you will NEVER hesitate to use it. You shoot whoever first and ask questions later. Do you understand?" she asked with a stern look.

I nodded and looked at the gun. I had never held one in my hands before. My hands quivered a little when I picked it up.

Tan stood up. "I will be your instructor for that course", he said as he pointed to the gun.

I met with Reina and our four Governors every day for two years. I learned about the organization, did visits to the parlors and clinics, did walk thrus of the real estate, met the distros, sampled the table courses, visited with the clients and picked up money.

Reina branded the rules in my head and they became bible to me. It didn't take me long to catch on and before I knew it, I became my title- Madam Summer. At twenty years old I was one rich bitch.

11 COMPETITION

The sound of the phone jolted me out of my sleep. "Hello, I said", sleepily. The voice on the other end sounded angry.

"Summer, meet me in the foyer. We have a problem", Reina said in her business voice. I knew the tone of her voice meant that I needed to get there quickly. I jumped out of bed and grabbed my robe as I headed out of my bedroom door.

I walked swiftly down the hallway and down the stairwell until I reached the foyer. As soon as I walked through the door of the foyer I saw Blue, Black, and Tan. They rose to their feet in my approach. The Governors only visited for meetings or major problems. We didn't have a meeting scheduled so that meant that the problem was even bigger than I thought.

It was customary for the Governors to rise upon my, or Reina's, entrance or exit. Every man below Governor was to bow and wait for instruction. We sampled all courses prior to their start of employment and it was considered a privilege to be able to pleasure us. It was a spot that was often competed for. Occasionally, we would get excellent reviews from customers at our tables and select those courses to pleasure us.

"You may be seated gentlemen", I said in my business voice. "What is the meaning of this unscheduled meeting?" I asked in a very aggravated tone.

Tan answered, "It appears that one of our clinics is losing patients. A few months back I informed Madam Reina about a problem with a clinic and neighboring clinic that does not belong to us. The Key Holder left a card and we delivered it to Madam for instruction".

I looked at Reina who looked pissed. "Well?" I asked. "How do you want to handle this?"

Reina glared at me and slid the business card across the table. When I picked it up. I saw the familiar name-TJ. He was the competition. Now shit was starting to make sense to me. That is why Reina was so angry when he came to deliver to Mama, he was serving in her territory.

"Well Summer, I don't have to ask you if you remember that Black ass Bill Nye the Science Guy muthafucka. I can see from that dumb ass smirk on your face that you definitely do", she snarled. "Handle him, or I will", she said as she got

47

up and stormed out.

The Governors stood up. "Tan, arrange a meeting for tonight with him. We'll use the private suite in the Table on North. 7:30 pm; you're dismissed", I told them as I was exiting the room.

I went back to my room and was going to order a snack, but decided against it because I wasn't sure just how I needed to handle TJ. Hmmm… I had an idea. On one of my trips to one of the Tables I met a visitor named Trice. She was the perfect pick to help pull off a plan with TJ.

Trice

I started thinking back to meeting Trice. She was a beautiful Black girl with brown eyes and full, beautiful lips. She was about five foot seven, slim build, but big busted with a small ass. She had a flat stomach with a tiny waistline. She wore long black straight weave to the middle of her back, and appeared to be kind of shy with socializing during the meeting. What stuck out the most to me was her comfort level during her session.

She came to the Table with a married couple, a man and a woman. The couple appeared to be a seasoned, settled married type. Trice didn't speak much at all, she let the couple do most of the talking. The husband ordered a snack for Trice and his wife. He decided he would watch.

When the snack was served I watched him pick Trice up to eat her pussy, he started to suck her titties and she moaned, the wife seemed jealous and entered the engagement by beginning to finger Trice. She kissed Trice's lips and her ears, then her neck. Trice became more excited and started to play with the snack's dick.

The snack started to eat Trice's pussy and Trice moaned in excitement, clutching his head. It drove the wife crazy and she pushed him off Trice to take over eating her pussy. The husband got up to unbuckle his pants and after he pulled them down he kneeled over Trice to put his dick into her mouth. She sucked his dick and became more aggressive with the sucking as the wife licked her pussy. The snack was escorted from the room, but I stayed to watch.

The husband pulled his dick out of her mouth and went behind his wife, pulling her skirt up and inserting his dick into her pussy while she continued to eat Trice's pussy. They moaned so intensely that it excited me. The husband watched her while he fucked his wife. Her movements were so sexy and you could see that the husband and wife both desired her more than each other.

At the end of the session I introduced myself to the customers and privately exchanged numbers with Trice. I inquired about her relationship to the couple. She told me that they were the first she'd engaged with as a couple and that she'd had many other experiences set up through the husband, including two men before; many the wife had no idea about.

She was way freakier than she looked. Her shy, innocent demeanor was what most attractive and intriguing about her. I knew that one day I'd want to fuck her too. I couldn't resist the urge to crave the feeling she gave to the couple. She knew it too, and the chemistry between us was insane. The wife felt it and did not like it. She quickly gathered her husband and Trice and left.

I picked up my cell phone and went through the call log. I dialed her number and waited. After about three rings, she picked up, "Summer, hi!" she said excitedly.

I talked to Trice for about an hour, just shooting the shit. Her voice was still as sweet as I remembered. I also knew that she would not be one that could say no easily, so it would be a piece of cake to get her to do what I needed done.

After about an hour into the conversation, I said, "Trice, I'd like to pay you to fuck a friend of mine. I need to do some persuading and I think you'd get the job done. You seem like a girl that likes to have fun".

In my mind, there would be an awkward silence. But, there was not. It wasn't even a minute before she responded, "I'm down".

As soon as I hung up with Trice the phone on my dresser rang. "Hello?" I answered. It was Luis on the other line.

"Miss Summer, the meeting has been scheduled", he stated and disconnected the call. I knew that TJ would accept the meeting. There was a weird chemistry between us when we met. I was sure that he would be just as curious as I was.

I went into the closet to find something that would make me look persuading. I found the perfect Alexander Wang lace bodysuit and blazer with a black Alexander Wang leather mini skirt and my black thigh high Louboutins. I pulled out a hot pink lace Fredrick's of Hollywood panty and bra set. My titties would show through the lace of the bodysuit and bra, so he'd have a clear view of my perfect nipples.

As I ran my bath I began to think about the plan. Trice was definitely going to help me win TJ over. But I needed a backup plan in the event he did not want to fall in line with the business. Reina's rules were straight forward and it would not be a smart idea for anyone to deny an allegiance to our organization. I also knew that Reina was already aggravated as fuck with TJ and she would not hesitate to put a bullet in his dome. What would be my back up plan?

I didn't let it wonder in my thoughts too long. I was too excited about the fun I would get to have in a business setting. I hoped into the bath tub and slid down while I soaked in deep thought.

My mind wondered to Mama. I hadn't spoken to her since I had left and I was a little worried about her. Reina always seemed aggravated whenever I mentioned Mama. It had started to come to the point that I stopped mentioning her just to not have to hear Reina's smart ass comments. That also meant I wasn't thinking about her anymore. I made a promise to myself that I'd go over to see her when I got some time. I wanted to drop off some money and make sure she was well. I knew that Mama knew how to survive, she had been doing that since before I was born. But, I still missed her and worried about her from time to time.

I leaned back into the tub and closed my eyes. About 20 minutes into my relaxing, I heard my cell phone ring. "Shit, can I have a fucking minute to myself?" I screamed out as I got up and stepped out the bath tub wet. I walked out of the bathroom into the bedroom and grabbed my cell phone.

"Hello?!" I said in an agitated tone. "Summer", the familiar tone answered back. "It's Ro", he began. "How are you?"

Suddenly my tone relaxed and I began to smile. It had been a minute since I'd heard from Ro and now that I was talking to him I realized I missed him.

"I'm good, how are you?" I asked him. "Good, now that I'm talking to you. What have you been up to?" he asked.

"Well, I've moved in with Reina" I replied. "Yea, I know", he said.

How the hell did he know that I moved in with Reina? Reina was super private so I know she hadn't told him and I hadn't had the time to talk to him.

"You know? How?" I asked, anxiously awaiting his reply. "Oh, I mean, word around the hood was that you moved out of the hood. I just assumed", he said in a trailed off voice.

"Oh, yea. Everything is good", I said. "Summer, I need to talk to you about something" Ro said. "Ok, well it will have to wait. I was right in the middle of a bath and I standing here wet" I replied.

"Can you meet me for dinner tomorrow night?" Ro asked. "Sure, text me the info, bye", I said as I hung up.

I went back to the bath and finished cleaning myself up. I got out and pulled out my smell goods. The evening was creeping up and it would be time for me to leave soon. I started lotioning up my body and then I picked up the phone on the desk to call Luis.

"Yes, Miss Summer", Luis answered in his thick accent. "Send a car for Trice", I responded and provided him the address. I wanted to make she would be in the car when I got in so that I could go over the plan with her.

I slipped on my clothing and sat at the vanity table to fix my hair and my makeup. I parted my hair in the middle and brushed it back into a neat, long, straight ponytail. I pulled out my hot pink lipstick from the Crayola Case and gave myself a Smokey eye. I gave myself a once over in the mirror and a nod of approval, then I jotted out the door and down the hall to wait for my car.

When I got downstairs Reina was seated in the library with a snack on his knees at her side. I went into the library and sat down. "I have a plan Rei, I'd prefer to keep TJ alive", I said.

Reina gave me a look of great thought and responded, "Ok, Summer, deal with him. But if I have to deal with him I'll do it my way". "You look scrumptious, if you can't convince him looking like that, he can't be convinced", she giggled.

I smirked at her and Luis interrupted our girlish giggles. "Your car has arrived Madam Summer", he stated.

I leaned over and kissed Reina on her cheek and exited the library.

As I was walking to the car I saw Trice standing outside of the door with a smile of excitement on her face.

She looked amazing. She was dressed in a black & white plaid school girl type mini skirt with black suspenders attached and white thigh high socks. She had on a white collar shirt with it unbuttoned to show her cleavage. Her titties sat up perfectly; and she had on black stiletto heels to match.

She had a neat, straight, jet black weave in with a part in the middle. The hair extended to her ass. Her perfect lips were glossy, her eye lashes neat, and her eyebrows were perfectly shaped.

When I reached the car, she leaned in to hug me. After a brief hug, the driver opened the door for us to get in.

As we got in the car I got right to business. I gave Trice a quick overview of my first encounter with TJ and what I needed from him. She didn't seem worried, surprised, or anxious at any of the information I gave her. I told her the expectation was that she would fuck him, but I would join in depending on the circumstance. I went over in details all of the scenarios I had come up with and how I wanted to see them play out.

We chopped it up for about an hour. After we talked about the plan, we went into casual conversation about life.

Trice told me about her background and the couple. She went on to tell me she was in a relationship with some other guy and how they met.

I listened to her more than talked about myself. This was a trait that I had inherited from Reina.

As Trice was talking I let the driver's window up for privacy, then I rubbed my hand up her skirt. She got quiet immediately. She didn't move or look uncomfortable. Instead, she opened her legs. I pulled her panties to the side and I stuck my two fingers in her pussy. She gasped in a small excitement and it made my panties wet. I kissed her neck as I fingered her pussy. She moaned.

She rubbed her hands on my titties and shoved my hand further into her pussy. I fingered faster and she started to groan. Just as she was about to cum on my fingers, I pulled them out. "Save it", I said, and pulled her skirt back down.

She smirked at me and went back to the conversation we were in. That's what I liked about her. I was attracted to the "fun" element that she had to her. It made me want her even more. There was no way I'd be able to have just one encounter to her. I wanted to keep her. I wanted her to be a part of my personal snacks. I knew I'd come back to that thought once we were done with this TJ situation.

We arrived at the parlor where we were meeting TJ. The driver sat awaiting my permission to disturb me. I opened the driver's window and nodded.

He exited the car and came around to open my door. I stepped out and Trice followed behind. We were met by two of the distros, who escorted us into The Table North back though the private suite. As soon as we walked through the doors of the suite. I laid eyes on TJ.

This man was a god and he looked gorgeous. He stood to his feet in his white collar button up, black khaki pants, and black ostrich Salvatore Ferragamos. His cologne filled the room. I could literally see his dick print protruding through his pants and I could feel my panties wet already.

I glanced at Trice and I could see there was excitement mounting in her too as she grabbed my hand. She gave my hand a small squeeze and I knew that she felt the exact same way about him as I did.

When I approached him he extended his hand for mine. I gave him my hand and he kissed it, "Miss Summer", he said with a smile that showed his gorgeous white teeth. He reached out to do the same to Trice.

"It's a pleasure to see you again", I said in a very stern tone. "This is Trice", I said, as he kissed her hand. "Please sit down", I said as I motioned for them both to sit on the expensive leather couches.

"I don't want to waste your time, so I'll get right to business", I said. "We want to do business with you, but I've heard you're not cooperating". I said as I gave him a warm smile. "I was hoping that I can convince you to change your mind. I've bought you a peace offering", I continued looking at Trice.

TJ sat back and crossed one of his legs over the other. He thought about his response for a moment, then he replied, "I'm not so sure about you wanting to do business *with* me. It seems more of a hostile takeover", he said.

"I assure you we are not a hostile organization", I said as I looked at Trice. She stood up and walked over to the couch where TJ was sitting. She started to unbutton her shirt.

I watched his eyes light up. She must have given him the same feeling she was giving me as I watched her.

When she her shirt was unbuttoned she slid it off her shoulders. I could see the red laced bra that showed her nipples. I could also see TJ's print harden up.

Trice unzipped her skirt in the back and pulled it down. Her red laced thong panties with the connected garner showed. Her body looked amazing and I had to force myself to have some self-control.

TJ uncrossed his legs and sat up. He pulled her in between his legs and rubbed his hand down between her breasts and over her belly. Trice looked at him and she didn't blink.

I sat back in a more relaxing position, to enjoy the show.

TJ began to lick Trice's belly and nibble on her thighs. He rubbed his hand slowly on her ass cheeks as he licked and nibbled. Then he pulled her panties down. She arched her back in a welcoming position between his grasp and he lifted her up onto the couch.

She let out a moan as she kneeled with him seated between her legs on the couch. He picked her so that her knees were on the top of the couch and he was positioned with his head between her legs and he pulled her down onto his face. I could see him insert his tongue into her pussy from my seat and she pushed her pussy down to his face in excitement.

She began to move her body on his face as if she were slowly riding a bull, careful not to fall off. She moaned and he moaned a muffled moan from beneath her. He kept his hands attached to her hips as she rode his face and she kept her hands mounted to the wall in front of her.

I got up from my seat and lifted my skirt. I pulled my panties down and stepped out of them as I headed over to the couch where they were.

I unbuttoned TJ's pants and attempted to pull them down. He lifted his bottom without moving Trice from his mouth and I slid his pants and underwear down. I started to suck his dick and he lifted Trice up and let out a groan of pleasure.

I played with the tip of his dick on my tongue and ran my hand from the bottom, near his balls, to the top near the tip where my tongue was adding a layer of moisture to it. He tried grabbed my head with one hand and held Trice on his mouth with the other.

She continued to ride his face speeding up the pace in extreme excitement as she moaned out in pleasure. She let out a squeal and she lifted enough for me to see the cum leak from her pussy onto his face.

TJ lifted her down and placed her over the couch. I lifted my mouth off of his dick to allow him to move freely. Trice slid off the couch and got on her hands and knees on the floor. He crawled behind her and mounted inside of her as he unbuttoned his shirt.

I crawled around Trice and slid underneath her just enough to expose my pussy near her mouth. She dived in and began to lick my pussy. I moaned and TJ fucked her harder as he leaned over her in an attempt to rub on me.

Our eyes locked and stayed that way as Trice ate my pussy causing me extreme pleasure. TJ fucked her harder as I became more aroused.

Just as I was about to cum. Trice inserted her fingers into my ass and I called out in excitement, "Ahhh, yeeesss." TJ leaned his head back at the sound of my cry to orgasm and he let out a squeal of excitement from the pleasure that Trice's pussy was giving him. At that very moment we all moaned out in excitement and each of us let off in orgasm.

TJ collapsed in exhaustion and Trice stood up, reaching her hand to help me up.

As she helped me to my feet a waitress appeared with a cleaning bucket and passed it to Trice. Trice got on her knees in front of me and sat the bucket on the side of her.

I stood with my legs opened, watching TJ as Trice cleaned me. She held my panties as I stepped into them and she pulled them up, adjusting my skirt to ensure my appearance was neat.

TJ had his eyes closed the entire time and he was clearly satisfied. When Trice was done cleaning me she cleaned herself and re dressed herself.

I sat down on the chair and Trice sat of the couch adjacent from me and we waited in silence as TJ recomposed himself. He stood up and put his dick back in his pants, buckled up his shirt, tucked his shirt into his pants, and sat down.

"Summer, you really are very convincing. I can see you have a lot of Maddy in you", he said. What the fuck did he mean by that?! My mind flashed back to the day we met and the sense that he knew me somehow.

"Really, and how do you know that?" I asked suspiciously. He smiled and replied, "She's been a client for quite some time and I've had the pleasure of meeting her in more ways than one."

So, he had been a client of Mama's. That had to be what he meant by *knowing* her. Or was it?

"I didn't come here to talk about my mother. I came here for business. Are you in or what?" I asked.

TJ stood up and headed toward the door. He turned to me and said, "I'll have to think about my options", as he exited the private suite.

I didn't get the outcome that I had hoped for, but it didn't mean that my plan had failed. But would Reina see it that way? She was already out of patience with him and I just didn't know if I had much time to do any more convincing.

I stood up to exit the suite and head back to the house. I motioned Trice to follow me as I exited the suite. When I exited the suite the distros were waiting to escort me back to my car.

When we got in the car I directed the driver to drop Trice at home and Trice and I made small talk to fill the time. We must have been driving for about thirty minutes when the car started slowing to a stop. I looked out to see that we were in my old hood. Trice lived in my old hood? How hadn't I known her?

We pulled up to her apartment building and the driver came around to let her out. "Summer, I hope to do this again with you sometime soon", she said as she smiled at me. "Next time, it'll just be you and me" I said, returning the smile. The driver escorted Trice to the door of her apartment building and I realized she lived a few blocks from my old high school. Everybody in the hood went to the same high school. It was weird that I had no idea who she was.

I didn't think too much of it as the driver returned to the car and started heading home.

A HOT SUMMER

12 THE FAMILIAR VOICE

Since it was going to be such a long ride home I decided to call Ro and chop it up. It would pass the time and I really missed him so it would be nice to catch up.

I dialed his number but he didn't answer. I left him a quick message just telling him that I called and to hit me when he had a moment. He usually never went too long without calling me back.

After I hung up the phone I leaned my head back and closed my eyes. The feeling of exhaustion took over me and I fell asleep. I dreamed of Ro and fucking him.

The dream seemed so real and I could smell him. This was not my normal dream. I didn't just dream of the sex, I was dreaming of laying up with him, smiling, and looking into his eyes.

Oh shit, I was in love with this nigga. The number one rule that Reina had in place, I had broken. I was in love with Ro. I started to think back to all the times I would see him with other girls and the small tinge of jealousy; that's when I realized, I had been in love with Ro.

I always knew that he loved me, but for the first time I was unsure if he felt the same way about me that I realized I felt about him.

I had fucked plenty of niggas and never became attached, I mean, I love the feeling of a phenomenal orgasm. How had I fallen in love with Ro?

I jumped and the jolt woke me from my sleep. I checked my phone and there was no missed call from Ro. It had never been a time that I called him and he didn't return my call.

What the fuck was this all about? Or was I tripping because now I had emotional baggage?

I glanced out the window and I could see that it had become dark out and we still hadn't reached the house. "How much longer before we're at home?" I asked the driver through the window.

"Madam Reina asked me to take you to the Table South to do a quality check", the driver responded.

I immediately became aggravated. Who the fuck did Reina think she was to change my destination without talking to me?! Reina had a bad habit of doing shit like that. I was not about to be treated like an employee. I was a partner.

"No, take me home, now, no need to inform her of the change of plans", I said. The driver looked worried but he got off on the upcoming exit and turned around.

I decided that I would give Reina a piece of my mind when I got home. I was too exhausted to deal with her and her attitude. I was also too tired from the TJ visit to do a check on shit. Reina had to know that I would be putting my all into this deal. Why would she schedule anything else for me tonight?

We drove for about fifteen minutes and I would see we were pulling up to the gate of our neighborhood. Once we entered into the gate and got near the front of the house's entrance I leaned up to the driver; "You can let me out here, I'd like to walk the rest of the way, and it'll give me time to enjoy the weather. You may go home for the night".

The driver pulled over and came around to open the door and help me out of the car. I stepped out to the smell of the beautiful garden at the entryway of the house. The driver closed the door, got in the car, and made a u turn to exit the property.

I sat down on the fountain and pulled off my boots. I sat there looking at the moon and the stars in the sky for a few moments, enjoying the weather. I was going to take a walk through the garden, but decided I just wanted to bathe and go to sleep so I headed toward the house. I still had to deal with Reina and that would be exhausting by itself.

I headed up the walkway to the house's entrance. When I got up to the driveway I saw Ro's car in the driveway. "What was he doing here?" I thought. But, then it dawned on me. He was planning a surprise for me and that is why Reina had the driver take me somewhere else. I suddenly felt stupid for being angry with her and turned to walk back toward the garden.

As I was walking through the garden a thought popped into my head. "Oh shit, I need to bathe in case I have to fuck Ro tonight. I'll sneak in the house, take a bath, sneak out and call like I'm on my way", I thought.

I quickly ran up the driveway to the door of the house. I put my ear to the door to see if I heard anyone or anything. The house seemed quiet, so I cracked the door as quietly as I could, and snuck in.

I tiptoed upstairs toward my wing, but then I noticed, the house was completely silent. That was weird because the house was never *completely* silent.

I turned around and started heading toward Reina's room. As I got closer to Reina's door I could hear her moaning. "Well" I thought, "she must not be in on the surprise, she's clearly having a snack. I giggled to myself and was about to head toward my room when I heard a familiar voice say, "You like that don't you?"

It was the same voice I had heard in Reina's room before and I could not make it out clearly to see where I had heard it before. Out of curiosity I cracked Reina's door just enough so that I could peep in. I was dying to know who this secret was Reina was keeping from me. I was also intrigued and I wanted to watch him please her.

As I peeped into the crack of the door my heart dropped to the floor. Ro was seated on the bed and Reina was seated over him, riding his dick while he sucked her titties. I watched, I wanted to move, but I couldn't.

Reina leaned down and kissed him passionately as she was moving her body in a sensual back and forth motion on him. He moaned out when she took her tongue out of his mouth. I was paralyzed.

Ro picked Reina up without removing himself from her and turned her over to lay her in the bed; then he removed his dick from her and got on his knees to please her. She grabbed his head and she moaned, a sound that was not meant to hide how good he made her feel. I *knew* how good he made her feel because he had made me feel like that many times before.

I was angry, but still I did not move. I stood there, watching, weeping silently. How could Reina do this to me?! She knew how I felt about Ro and she was the main one always telling me to stay away from him.

I turned around and began to walk quickly to my room. My face was submerged in tears and my mind was clouded with anger. When I got to my bedroom door, I dropped to my knees and let the tears take over me. I cried for about fifteen minutes before I decided that I was more pissed than hurt.

I got up and went into my room. I picked up my cell phone and called Reina. "Hello?" she answered.

"You changed my direction without talking to me Reina", I said in a very firm tone.

"I figured since you were out you could take care of it", she replied. "You ok? You sound pissed", she said.

"I'm fine. Don't change shit unless you talk to me first", I said, and disconnected the call.

She tried calling me back about five times and I didn't answer. She sent me a text asking me what was up and to call her. I didn't respond.

I ran a bath and got in it. I leaned my head back prepared to go into my thoughts, but then my phone rang. I reached over to grab it and saw that it was Ro. He must have been done with Reina.

I picked up the phone, "Hello?" I answered. "Summer, hey, I'm sorry I missed your call. What are you up to?" he asked.

"Oh, nothing. I'm looking forward to dinner tomorrow night. I'm going to be your dessert course", I replied. Ro was silent for a moment. Then he said, "Summer, I miss you and I love you."

I literally looked at the phone. Did this muthafucka say he missed me and loved me?! He just got done fucking my best friend!" I was going to teach him a lesson.

"That's sweet", I replied, "see you tomorrow night", I said before I disconnected the call. I finished my bath and got into the bed. Just before I fell asleep I texted Reina that everything was fine and I had made it home, I would see her in the morning. Then I drifted off to sleep.

My dreams were like nightmares. I must have tossed and turned all night, seeing Reina and Ro fucking on repeat. I saw myself walking up behind them while their eyes were closed, enjoying the pleasure, and stabbing Reina in the back with a pair of scissors.

I jolted awake from my sleep and looked over at the alarm clock to see a two fifteen staring back at me. Shit, what was I going to do? If there was one thing I had learned from Reina, it was that I always had to have a plan. I decided that I was going to deal with them both, but I was going to start with Reina.

I picked up my cell phone, slid my blanket down, opened my legs, and snapped a picture of my pussy, making sure to get a clear shot of my clit. I found Ro in my contacts and sent it. I waited.

As if nothing had changed, he hit me right back with a tongue emoji. I texted him back a smiley face emoji and put my phone on the bedside desk.

I went back to looking at the ceiling and I lost myself in deep thought. I saw memory flashes of the first time I saw Ro and Reina's reaction. I went over all the times in my head that she had made some sort of snarky remark about Ro, especially when I told her how good he would fuck me.

It was evident all along. I just chose not to see it. I thought about all the lessons that Mama had taught me. Somehow along the way I had forgotten Mama's forbidden girlfriend rule, but held dear to Reina's rules. Reina had groomed me to be who she wanted me to be, and I had lost all sight of who I actually was.

But, I thought to myself, the end game was the same. Reina only accelerated my opportunity to my goal and I was not going to be stupid enough to ruin it. The fact was, I needed Reina. I needed all of her connections, to master the business, and my luxurious lifestyle, including the salary, that was provided to me as a partner.

I had to play the game the right way, which was the way to take over. I decided I was going to take Reina's spot. I'd study the business, the books, learn the spots, and let her open up to me completely, secure her love for me even more; and when I felt I was ready, I'd put a bullet in her head.

It's one thing that I knew for certain, Reina enjoyed feeling good as much as I did and that would be my way to unlock all of the barriers that she still had up. I had been with Reina for almost three years and I still felt like I didn't know anything about her.

Although she had opened up to me and trusted me more than anybody else, it was clear that Reina still had secrets. I needed to know it all. It was in those secrets that I would find her weakness, and that's how I would take her down.

The thought of Reina's take down put a definite smile on my face and that is how I fell back to sleep, smiling. I must have been in a deep sleep because I woke up to my phone ringing. By the time I rolled over to grab it, it had stopped and I saw that I had seventeen missed calls from both Reina and Ro.

What the fuck could they possibly want?!

13 CATCHING UP

I picked the phone up and pressed Reina's missed call and waited while it rang. Finally, she picked up. "Summer, hey", she said.

"Hey Rei, what's up? You ok?" I asked in an innocent, worried tone. Reina was silent for a minute and then she responded, "The driver said that he brought you back early last night." She let her voice trail off and I could definitely tell that she was wondering whether or not I had known that Ro was there.

"Yea, I was exhausted and irritated from the meeting and I got to the house, ran in, and immediately passed out", I said. "I thought you'd be able to tell by how snippy I was last night", I finished, with a chuckle.

Reina's entire mood lifted and she replied, "Oh, yea. I did catch that shitty mood" she said while laughing. I listened to her with a disgusted look on my face, but I didn't change the tone of my voice. Reina was certain that I didn't know Ro was in the house. She was clearly more relaxed and was busy cracking jokes about how the meeting must have went.

"Well, get dressed Sum and meet me in the foyer", Reina said. I really didn't want to see her at that very moment. I wasn't sure that I would be able to keep myself composed. "Rei, I'm still in the bed, let's do it later", I responded.

"Summmmerrrr, come on, I want to show you something", she said, as if we were still in high school. I could tell whatever it was, she was excited about it. "Ok, let me get dressed and I'll meet you in the foyer", I replied in a tired voice.

When I hung up the phone with Reina I dialed Ro's number. "Summer, hi", he answered. "Hello Roosevelt", I responded, "what's up?" It must have taken Ro by surprise because he started to stutter over his words.

"Uh, um, did I do something to upset you?" Ro asked. "Oh, no!" I said, realizing that I had to knock off the shitty attitude if I was going to carry out the plan. "Reina just woke me up and I'm a little cranky", I told him.

He laughed a little, a nervous laugh, "Oh, ok, I was just making sure. Are we still on for tonight?" Ro asked.

"I wouldn't miss it for the world" I replied. "I'll pick the place and text you the address, cool?" I asked.

"Miss Summer, always in control", Ro laughed, "sure, that's cool" he finished. I hung up and jumped up out the bed to find my clothes and turn on my shower.

Once I was out of the shower I grabbed a black velvet Burberry jogging suit, brushed my hair back into a long ponytail, threw on my Giuseppe gold bar sneakers and headed downstairs. I knew Reina wouldn't be happy. She hated when I dressed *hood* as she called it and always preferred me to be in dress code.

I glided down the hall, without a care, not even about what Reina might think or say. I was in control, she just didn't know it yet, but she would soon find out.

As I walked down the stairwell I could see Reina standing near the front door, smiling. She was standing with Luis, Black, and Tan. I returned the smile, wondering what all the cheerfulness was about.

"What are you so happy about?" I said as I got closer to Reina with a grin on my face. "Close your eyes, I want to show you something", she said. I looked at her for a moment, then I thought, *what the hell, it couldn't be any worse than finding her fucking the one man that I ever loved.* I closed my eyes and smiled.

Reina grabbed my hand and I heard the front door open. She led me outside and I was surprised by the immense amount of heat. I'd been so busy that I hadn't even noticed that summer had slipped up on us again.

"Go ahead, open your eyes", Reina yelled. When I opened my eyes I saw it; a black New Continental Range GT Bentley with black rims, chrome spikes, and a big red bow. My mouth dropped and I was lost for words.

"I know it's early, but I saw it and immediately knew you had to have it!" Reina said excitedly. "Happy Birthday Summer!" Reina, Luis, and the Governors yelled.

Shit! My birthday had crept up on me. I didn't even realize it was around the corner. I was about to be twenty one years old, but I felt like I was much older. Even worse, it had been three years since I'd seen or spoken to Mama.

"Oh my god, thank you Rei", I screamed and hugged her. I ran down to the car and opened the door. It had black leather seats, a moon roof, and the dash was lined with chrome. The driver seat had a stitching that read: *Madam Summer*

I sat in the seat and flipped down the visor which dropped the keys. I sat back and closed my eyes for a second. This car was beautiful and it was well deserved. This snake in the grass bitch felt guilty, as she should, and this would be the first of many extra expensive gifts, whether she knew it or not.

"I'm going to take it for a spin", I yelled out to Reina, and started the car up. It started up so quiet that I had to look at the dash to make sure it was on.

I started down the driveway and out of the neighborhood toward Mama's house. I hopped on the expressway and tested the power of the engine. I was in love with the car, the look, feel, and smell-all of it.

I grabbed my cell phone out of my pocket and dialed Ro. "Hi Summer", he answered. "Hey, I'm going by to see my mama, let's meet up when I leave there instead of dinner", I replied. "Sounds good, see you soon", Ro said and I disconnected the call.

As I drove, I enjoyed the scenery. Although I had seen it a million times before, this time it looked amazing. I was excited to be seeing Mama. Reina has always frowned at any thought from me of communicating with Mama, so I didn't. But now that things were changing, I realized that I needed another boss bitch in my corner; there was no better choice than Mama.

I exited the expressway into my old neighborhood and drove past my old high school. It looked so different. Someone had obviously put some money into it because it looked like a college campus. Pretty soon I pulled up to Mama's apartment.

On my way to the door I saw our old chairs from the kitchen next to the trash. "Summer, is that you?" a voice asked. I turned around to see the old nosey ass neighbor and apartment manager that had lived across the hall from us since I could ever remember. "Hi Candace, yea, it's me", I replied.

"Wow, look at you. It looks like you're doing well for yourself since you went off to college", Candace said. I didn't think too much of it. I was pretty sure it was some story Mama gave Candace to get her to mind her fucking business.

"Yea, it seems so", I replied as I returned to my walk to the apartment building's door. "Oh, you ain't looking for your Mama are you? I would have assumed she would have told you that she moved. What kind of mother moves away while their child is at college and doesn't even tell them?" she asked in her judgmental ass voice.

Trying not to sound too irritated, I responded, "Moved where? She had been calling me but I have been busy."

"Well let me see", she said as she was digging in her big raggedy purse. He left a business card and assured me that he would take care of the rent through the end of the lease. She pulled out a business card and handed it to me.

Salvador Gates, U.S Senate is what the card read, along with an address. Written neatly on the side was a note. Please send the bill to the addressee who will handle Madelyn Gate's affairs. On the back of the card was a number. I took my cell phone out of my pocket and dialed it as I headed back to the car.

Candace was talking but I drowned out what she was saying as I hopped in the car and pulled off.

"The Gates Residence", a voice answered. I was quiet. "Hello? The Gates Residence", the voice repeated.

"Hello, I'm looking for Maddy", I replied to the voice. "May I tell her who is calling?" the voice responded.

I hung up. I decided I'd just ride over to the residence. I needed to know what the hell Mama was doing with the US Senate and how were they related to us. I headed toward the address.

The drive was the same direction that Reina and I lived in so it seemed as if I was driving forever. When I finally turned into the neighborhood I realized exactly where I was. What the fuck was Mama doing at her parent's house?

Mama had described the house to me so vividly before that as soon as I knew the house without even looking at the address. The property was huge and there were multiple cars in the drive way of the main house. I pulled in behind one of the cars, parked, and shut the engine off.

It looked like they were having some sort of party. The windows were huge and the house had a very open architectural build. I literally could see right in the window from the car. There were a bunch of men and women dressed in suits and ties and expensive gowns. It was also a ton of wait staff walking around with trays that held food and Champaign.

There was no way that I could go up to the door in what I had on. It was the one time I wished I had listened to Reina about the dress code of a business woman. I decided if I saw Mama I would get her attention and have her meet me outside.

I watched the party for about forty five minutes before I saw her. The sight of Mama took my breath away. She was always stunningly beautiful, but she was something more. She was dressed in a black Alexander Wang gown with a train that followed. She had her hair pulled back and her beautiful green eyes shimmered behind the smoky eye. She wasn't walking, she was gliding as if she was on air. Seeing Mama look so beautiful brought tears to my eyes.

I didn't belong there. Mama was doing better than she had ever did without me. I started the car up and backed out the driveway. I glanced up at the window to get one last look at Mama and we locked eyes with each other.

Mama turned to head away from the window, probably toward my direction. I didn't stop, I continued backing out, turned around, and drove away. I didn't even look back in the mirror for fear of seeing Mama chasing after me and getting the urge to go back. Mama had suffered long enough because of me and I wasn't about to ruin her happiness.

I exited the neighborhood and called Ro. "Hey", he answered. "Hey, let's meet up at this place called the Table South. I'll text you the address. Wait for me outside and we'll go in together" I told him. "Cool" he responded and hung up.

I picked up the phone and dialed the house. Luis answered. "Make a reservation for me at the Table South, private dinner, no interruptions", I told him. "Yes, Madam", Luis replied in his thick accent.

I headed toward the Table South to meet up with Ro. I was about to put my plan of revenge into motion.

When I pulled up to the Table South I could see that Ro had already arrived and was waiting in his car as he was told. I hopped out and headed over to his car. Before I could get near his car, he hopped out with a big grin on his face.

"Summer!" he yelled out. I forced a smile and greeted him warmly. "Hi Ro", I said as he approached me with open arms. We embraced each other and the smell of his cologne turned me on. I suddenly felt butterflies in my stomach. I wasn't sure if it was because I was in love with him, or because I was nervous that he would be able to see what I had up my sleeve. Either way, I had already put the plan in motion or there was no turning back.

"Wow, I've never been here before, what do they serve?" Ro asked. "Well tonight it's serving me" I replied with a slight grin.

Ro chuckled and extended his arm with an invitation for me to hook mine into his as he escorted me to the door. I could clearly tell he didn't take me seriously and I was about to introduce him to a new world.

As we were walking to the door I leaned over and whispered, " I know Reina and I are private and sometimes it comes across that I am less interested in you than I really am, but tonight I want to let you into my world, and Reina's, so you will understand why I seem so distant."

Ro looked at me completely shocked and a slight look of nervousness showed through his facial expressions. "Wow, Summer, I never thought you wanted anything serious from me. I mean, I guess" he began to say before I cut him off. "No, it was never that. It was just, well Reina didn't think it was a good idea for me to get into a serious relationship with you. She didn't want me sharing our business life with you."

I could see the look of anger on his face. He was trying to contain it, but he wasn't being successful. "Reina, huh? Did she say why?" he asked.

"She did, but I don't want to hurt your feelings", I replied. Just as he was about to insist on me telling him, we arrived at the door.

We were greeted by the hostess and directed to our private dining area. As we came closer to our dining area Ro's facial expressions began to change. I could tell he was totally shocked by what he was witnessing. It was evident to him by that point that we were not at a regular restaurant.

When we reached our private dining area Ro looked at me and asked, "Summer, what's going on? What kind of place is this? It's obviously not a restaurant."

"Actually, it is. It's just the things served here satisfy a different type of appetite" I responded. "Welcome to my world; I was introduced into this a few years ago by Reina. You can imagine my surprise that my best friend since high school kept so many secrets from me. She didn't exactly give me a choice, she used the fact that I was the product of a coked out mama to draw me in."

Ro had a look of sadness and disgust on his face. "Summer, I'm so sorry" he said.

"Don't be Ro. Reina helped me learn to survive and I'm grateful for that. I know that she loves me and would never do anything to hurt me, just like I know that you wouldn't either" I responded.

His face went to complete sadness. He was about to say something but I leaned over and kissed him. The kiss was from the core of my soul. I did love this man, but he had hurt me, and he would pay.

Ro kissed me back, just as passionately and I rubbed my hand over his leg to his zipper. I unzipped his pants and then unbuckled them. I could feel his dick rock hard and I began to massage it through is underwear. He kissed my neck and my ear as I closed my eyes to enjoy the pleasure.

Just then, I heard the door to our dining area open. Ro jumped in nervousness, trying to pull away from my hand. I didn't stop and when he seen her his dick went on full erect and came from inside of his boxers.

Trice looked gorgeous. She had on a black lace panty and bra set. The lace was positioned to show a clear view of her beautiful nipples, and the cheeky panties, that displayed her smooth dark ass, and a view of her smooth, hairless pussy. She had on a garner that connected the panties to her thigh highs and some red stiletto pumps. Her hair was parted in the middle, brushed to the back in a long jet black ponytail.

Ro was astounded at her sex appeal and as I leaned over to nibble on his ear, I could hear his heart beating very fast. "Roosevelt, I'd like for you to meet Trice. She'll be joining us for dinner tonight" I whispered in his ear. I nodded at Trice and she came over to where we were seated on the couch.

She climbed on the couch with her body positioned over Ro's and began to lick his ear. I continued to massage his dick with one hand as I kicked off my shoes and pulled down my pants and panties with the other. Ro moaned soft sounds as Trice licked his ears and his neck and he rubbed her ass cheeks. I took Trice's free hand and I placed in on the spot where I was massaging Ro's dick and she took over.

I stood up and began to take my clothes off. Ro watched me as Trice continued to kiss on his neck and ears. She began to unbutton his shirt and by the time I was down to my panties and bra had removed his shirt and opened his underwear, pulled his dick up so that the full erect was ready to be sat on.

I leaned over as if I was putting my clothes on the chair and I dialed Reina's number. I sat the phone on the table next to the chair and I left it there.

I went up to where Trice was seated on Ro, massaging his bare dick and kissing his neck and ears, and I positioned myself in back of Trice. I began to kiss her neck and unbutton her bra. I pulled her straps down and rubbed her thighs. She moaned and I lifted her to pull her panties to the side as she was leaned over Ro so that her titty was on his mouth.

I immediately stuck my fingers in her pussy from underneath and started to finger her. She moaned and I kissed her back and rubbed her ass with my free hand. She let out a pleasure squeak and began to ride my fingers. I fingered her for a little while longer to give Ro enough time to enjoy the taste of her perfect, rounded titties, and then I lifted her off my fingers, pulled her panties to the side, and sat her on Ro's dick.

As I pushed her down onto his dick, she let out a sound of pleasuring pain.

I knew the feeling exactly. Ro had a big dick, and the first time sitting on it fully erect would be painful, at first. But, after you adjusted, every stroke would hit your G-spot.

Trice began to ride Ro's dick and he moaned. I crawled on the side of him and whispered, "Say my name"."

"Oh Summer, you are driving me crazy", he moaned. "I'm going to eat the shit out of your pussy", he said forcefully to me.

I said, "Yea, why do you want to eat my pussy Ro?" He responded, "Because I'm in love with you, always have been."

I pushed myself from behind Trice where she was riding Ro's dick and I crawled on the side of him on the couch. I laid his head back and then I stood up over him, positioned with my ass in Trice's face, but my pussy over his mouth, and then I squatted.

He placed his tongue on my clit, I moaned in extreme excitement, and Trice went crazy. She started riding Ro as if she were at a bull cage and she grabbed ahold of my ass, giving it small nibbles on the cheek as Ro ate my pussy. Ro moaned unable to contain himself and he licked my pussy as if he were looking for the center to the tootsie roll.

I began to ride his tongue and I grabbed my titties, pulling my nipples to grant me a pleasuring pain. And then I heard Trice, she groaned and grabbed my ass pushing me on Ro's tongue, causing it to insert inside my pussy walls. I yelled in pleasure and so did Trice, and then I felt it. It was as if entire soul met together and rushed out of my pussy. I lifted off Ro's mouth to see the serious thick, white, residue all over his mouth area.

70

Trice groaned and let out a yell just as deep as mine, right before Ro's groan of accomplishment. He yelled out, "Ohhhhhhhh, Summerrrrrrr, I'm about to cum!!!!" as if I was the one riding his dick like a bull, and he nutted in Trice.

I rolled over and fell on the couch in exhaustion, reaching for the phone on the table. "Dessert please" I told the answering party. A minute later waiter came through the door with and began to clean me up. When he was done cleaning me up, he handed a fresh bowl with cleaning utensils to Trice and exited the room.

As I was putting my clothes on I glanced at my phone and I could still see the numbers going, which meant that Reina was still on the phone. Her voicemail would have hung up by now.

I picked up my phone and looked at Trice and Ro. "Shit, I think I accidentally butt dialed Rei" I said. I put the phone to my ear, "Hello?" Silence. A minute later, there was a click. I turned to put my phone back on the table and when my back was turned to Ro and Trice, I smiled. Bitch.

After straightening myself out, I sat and watched Trice clean Ro up and couldn't help but let my mind wonder back to Reina. I could only imagine what she must have been thinking. I hoped she had the same feeling I did the night I saw her and Ro together.

It was an awkward silence in the room that had been there ever since I had brought up Reina's name. Ro hadn't said much, and Trice was always quiet when she was working so it wasn't surprising for her.

After Ro was dressed and seated, I asked, "You ok? You seem like it's something on your mind."

"No, I just realized that I promised my parents that I'd have dinner with them tonight and I totally forgot when I scheduled this *dinner* with you" Ro said. I knew he was lying. Since when did he give a shit about what his parents wanted him to do when it came to me?! It had never been a day that he didn't drop everything at the very sight of me! This definitely meant that he had feelings for Reina. I was sure that he was going to do damage control.

It didn't matter though. I already knew that my plan had been put into motion and I was separating myself from him emotionally. Ro had turned into business, just a tool used to get Reina.

"Oh, do you need to go?" I asked innocently. While he thought about it I sat back and crossed my legs as if anticipating a yes to the question I'd just asked.

"Yea, I'm a get going. How long before you make it home?" he replied. This nigga was trying to gage my time out of the house so that he could run to her! "It'll probably be a few hours" I responded. He got up, came over to where I was sitting and kissed me on my forehead before he exited the suite. I gave him a smile, but deep down inside I was already disgusted.

Once Ro was gone I chopped it up with Trice. We talked about the experience with Ro and how he gave her multiple orgasms because his dick was so big. Trice did most of the talking. I listened and smiled every now and then to show here I was engaged in the conversation. However, my mind was lost in the thoughts of Reina and Ro. I imagined all of the things he must have been thinking, including the fact that I had laid on him deciding not to be in a relationship with him was all her idea. I had also explained all of Reina's business to Ro. He must have felt like a damn fool at the thought that Reina had kept so many secrets. I mean, she was fucking him. Yet, she didn't even trust him enough to invite him into her world.

The thought of hurt that she had to feel crossed my mind and for just a second I felt sad for her. After all, she was my best friend. She had given me a life that I was groomed to have without a nigga. I quickly snapped out of it. It was the same bitch that had also tried to keep me away from the nigga that I loved so she could have him for herself.

Who knew what else Reina was up to? She was always so damn secretive. The fact was, Reina could have an ulterior motive for me and I would never know. I had trusted her fully, but she had only trusted me to a certain point. Even after years of knowing her, she still hadn't fully opened up to me. Yet, she knew everything about me. It's one thing I could definitely admit, she had gave me some lessons that I would use to burn her ass.

I called for Trice a ride and when it arrived the Distro and I walked her out to meet her driver. I thanked her, paid her, and felt her up one last time. Although I had told Ro it would be a few hours before I got home, it was definitely time to go home.

14 AWKWARD EMOTIONS

On the ride home I decided to call Ro, just to see if he would answer. One ring, two rings, three rings.

"Hello, you have reached Roosevelt. I'm unable to get to my phone. Please leave a message."

I hung up and texted him, *"Hey, how did that thing go with your parents?"*

I waited, no response. Unable to control it, I became pissed. I could barely wait until we reached the house and saw his car there. This time I would bust into Reina's room and catch them together. Shit was going to get ugly.

As we got closer to the house my heart began to beat faster. It wasn't fear, it was anger. There was an indescribable adrenaline rush.

When we finally arrived, Ro's car was not in the driveway. It gave me a small sense of relief. Maybe he was over Reina once and for all.

I went into the house and I headed upstairs toward Reina's room. On the way to her room I ran into Luis.

"Madam Summer, if you're looking for Madam Reina she is not here" he said in his extra thick accent.

"Where is she?" I asked Luis. "I don't know. She asked for a car and left out the door abruptly. Perhaps something went wrong at one of the businesses. She seemed highly aggravated and angry" he responded.

"Thank you Luis" I said and dismissed him. I picked up my cell phone to call Reina. After four rings, just when I thought the voicemail would pick up, Reina answered.

"Rei, hey! I think I butt dialed you earlier. Where are you?" I asked. Reina paused for a moment and then in her normal stern voice she responded, "I am on my way back. I had an emergency meeting with the Governors and distros. We met with TJ."

"Wait, why didn't you tell me?" I asked Reina in dissatisfaction. "It was nothing that I needed to interrupt you from. I figured you were servicing a client from the sounds of it. I didn't want to interrupt you. It was something that I was able to handle" Reina said. "Let's have dinner tonight, I want to share the good news. I'll be there shortly" she said before hanging up the call.

I didn't have time to think about Ro. I was stuck on TJ. What kind of agreement had they come to when I wasn't around? It's obvious I had given him a very hard to resist deal, including Trice. He hadn't bent. Now all of a sudden he was down? What the hell was going on?!

I waited for Reina to get there. The minutes seemed to drag by waiting for her arrival. I started to pace the floor in the foyer in anxiousness. Finally, I saw lights from a vehicle coming up the driveway. I quickly went into the library and grabbed one of our business books. I made myself look as if I was reviewing the finances when Reina finally walked in.

"Hey" I said as I got up and met her for a kiss on the cheek, our usual embrace. There was no sign of aggravation or anger on Reina's face. She seemed normal. She returned the embrace and sat across from me on the couch.

"Great news! TJ has decided to join the organization" she said without much enthusiasm.

"How? What did you do? I couldn't get a straight answer from him even after serving him" I spat out.

"I made him a deal he couldn't resist. He will get his own territory of his choice and we will only ask for 33% as long as we are the sole distributor of product" she said casually.

"Why the fuck would you cut a deal like that?! That is something that we would never do" I said to her angrily.

"Summer, there is nothing that we would NEVER do. In this business, I'll do what I have to do to get what I need done. Keep that in mind" she said as she stood up from her seat.

"I've had the Chef prepare us dinner. I'm famished! Let's eat" she said in her excited voice, exiting the room toward the kitchen.

I followed her in disbelief. I wasn't sure what was going on with Reina, but I knew whatever it was could not be good. She was acting bat shit crazy. She had just give TJ a consistent half a million dollar business, after our cut. Every lesson she had ever taught me was about NOT doing something so damn stupid.

Yet, she somehow managed to go and fuck up money on her own.

As we sat at the dining table and ate, Reina chatted happily about how well business was doing. I shared some experiences with Trice and Reina was intrigued. She definitely wanted to have a go round with Trice in the near future.

We talked about expenses and she started in on how she wanted us to spend more time together. Somehow she felt that she had let business build a distance between us and she wanted to nourish our sister ship.

There were so many moments where I felt like I wished I had never walked in to find her with Ro. But, there were also many moments where I felt like I couldn't trust her and I wanted to kill her. The entire dinner conversation was very awkward for me and I had to hide the awkwardness.

I knew Reina could tell when something was wrong. I caught her staring at me several times throughout the dinner, but she never addressed it. She just continued to talk and laugh, occasionally cracking jokes.

It was a weird type of comfort to have Reina back to her old self. This was the Reina that I had been privy to before I was introduced to the business. This was the Rei that I loved and I desperately wanted my friend back. I wanted to trust Reina and the lessons that she had taught; especially, one of the most important- *never let your emotions cloud your judgement in business*.

"Summer, I love you, thank you for being my best friend. I just want to say, if there is ever anything I did to hurt you I am truly sorry" Reina said suddenly, with a very concerning look on her face.

My mind stopped drifting off at the sound of her words. I looked at her in the face and responded, "Rei, I love you too. You're my best friend. There is nothing you could ever do to change that."

Bitch.

Reina smiled at me and went back to talking as if it had never been said. I paid close attention to her facial expressions and body language, looking for any sign that she was not genuine. It didn't seem to be any.

I wondered if she saw my lack of genuineness when I responded to her. Rei had always been very good at reading me. In her business she had to be good at reading people. It was how she survived and became the Head Bitch in Charge.

When we were done with dinner, Rei walked me to my room. After we reached my door she leaned over and embraced me. "Goodnight, let's do breakfast in the morning lazy bones" she said.

I smiled and entered my room closing the door behind me.

What the fuck was up with Reina? Had hearing me fucking Ro, or Ro telling me he loved me drove her crazy?

I slipped out of my clothes, climbed in my bed, and grabbed my phone to see if Ro had called me back. Nothing. He hadn't returned my call or my text. It had been hours since I had called and texted him. This was some bullshit. It was obvious he wasn't with Reina.

After a couple hours of waiting for Ro to call me back, I drifted off to sleep. I had dreams of Reina's crazy ass behavior and visions of her being with Ro before she came home. Needless to say, my sleep was restless.

It seemed like I was sleep for an hour when the sun peeped through my drapes. I opened my eyes and rolled over to grab my phone. Nothing.

Ro had not called or texted me back. My heart began beating fast enough to imitate a heart attack. Had he chosen Reina over me?!

I wasn't sure if the feeling that I felt was heart break or anger, but it definitely jolted my body in the upright position. I grabbed my cell phone and I called him again. The phone rang over and over, then the voicemail. I called him several more times, but he didn't answer.

I don't think I had ever called anyone, as many times as I had called him, in my life. I sent him a couple texts asking him to hit me right back under the notion that it was important. He didn't.

I picked up the desk phone and I dialed Reina's room. She picked up, "Hey, you up already?' she asked sleepily.

"Go back to sleep. We can eat when you get up" I said following it up with a fake laugh.

Ok, Reina wasn't with Ro. Who the fuck was he with that was more important than me?!

I thought about calling down for a snack to help take my mind off of Ro, but I wasn't feeling it. I was starting to feel sick to my stomach. I had never had this feeling before and I didn't like it.

I laid down on my pillow and I cried silently. I cuddled my pillow as if he was next to me and I sobbed for the next forty five minutes. It must have worn me out because I drifted off to sleep again.

I woke up to a knock on the door. "Come in" I answered, not bothering to get out of the bed.

"You're still in the bed?!" Reina said jokingly. "Come on, let's eat. I'm starving. Come in your pajamas, I don't want to wait for you to get dressed" she said as she exited my room.

I waited about ten minutes and I hopped out the bed, went to the bathroom, brushed my teeth, and washed my face.

I headed downstairs to the kitchen.

Reina was already seated at the breakfast bar and had started to eat with the television on, listening to the news. The butler and one of the housekeepers were standing off to the side awaiting any order and Luis was seated at the kitchen table reading a newspaper.

Reina motioned me to come sit down where a plate was already awaiting my arrival along with a glass of juice. I sat down and begin to eat when the news reporter's words hit me like a ton of bricks.

Police are actively seeking any information regarding the whereabouts of Roosevelt Carson whose car and cellphone were found abandoned on Interstate 25 last evening. Authorities described the sight as a possible crime scene and have no leads at this time. His parents are offering a $50,000 reward with any information leading to the safe return of their son.

"Omg!" I screamed. Reina did not even look up or seemed bother my screams. She continued to eat her breakfast.

"Reina, Ro is missing!" I screamed again as I was shaking her.

"Oh shit!" Reina said, "That is so fucked up. It's a cold world" she finished as she returned to eating.

I looked at Reina in total disbelief. She didn't even acknowledge the awkward silence or look up to see me looking at her in disgust. She just continued to eat her breakfast, as if she was starving, and drink her coffee.

I turned to look at Luis and he hadn't even looked up from the newspaper. I felt like I was in a fucking twilight zone.

"Summer, sit down and eat! Aren't you hungry" Rei asked, when she finally looked up. "Why are you being so extra? I mean you fucked the nigga a time or two, but as far as I know, it wasn't anything different. Muthafuckas disappearing every day. Why are you so bent out of shape over this one?" she asked casually and rhetorically.

What the fuck did this Bitch do with Ro?

She was fucking evil and crazy; and I was scared. "I'm not hungry" I said as I quickly headed toward the exit of the kitchen. As I turned around, I caught a glimpse of her shrugging her shoulders and reaching over to grab bacon off my plate.

Crazy Bitch.

When I was out of Reina's sight, I started to cry. My gut told me that she had something to do with whatever happened to Ro. I didn't know what to do. I was terrified. There had been many times that I'd been unsure of who Reina was because she was so secretive, but at this point, it was evident that she didn't give a fuck. She would not hesitate to make anyone that she felt crossed her, disappear.

I cried all the way to my bedroom. When I got into my room I climbed in my bed under my covers and cried some more. I was physically sick to my stomach at the thought of something horrible happening to Ro. I leaned over, grabbed the waste basket, and threw up in it. I was scared and I wished for Mama.

I pulled myself out of the bed and to the bathroom where I ran my shower. I can't win if I'm weak.

I gotta get my shit together. Reina wins because she doesn't have a weakness. I can't have one either.

I let the water run off my back as thoughts ran through my head. I needed to get a grip on my emotions. I was vulnerable to her as long as I made decisions based off emotions. I wanted to call Mama, she would know what to do. She had survived in the game way longer than I had, but she was in a good place in life and I couldn't bring myself to ruin it. This would be something that I had to figure out on my own.

I needed something to clear my mind so I could think straight. I got out of the shower and wrapped myself in a towel. I headed to the desk phone and picked it up. "Luis, send me a quick bite to eat please" I said before I hung up.

A few moments later a knock on my door and when I opened it, he was everything I needed to help clear my head.

Luis handed me the leash and I closed the door, then I unleashed him. "What is your pleasure Madam?" he asked as he kneeled at my feet.

"Hurt me" I said and dropped my towel.

He picked me up off the floor and threw me on the bed before crawling over me as if he were a hunting lion. He bit my nipples painfully and grabbed my hips to leave bruises. He forced his four fingers into my pussy before I was turned on enough to moisturize and I cried out in pain.

When I cried out he grabbed my throat with his other hand and told me to shut up. His grasp on my neck was too tight and I struggled to tell him. When I stopped trying to talk he released my neck and continued forcing his fingers in and out of my pussy. The pain turned to pleasure and I began to moan.

He pulled all four fingers out of my pussy and backed up off me. Then, he lifted my bottom and began to lick my pussy roughly. His tongue was so wet and warm and I was turned on. He paused several times to bite my ass checks which was very painful, yet I was overwhelmed by pleasure the second he returned to licking my pussy.

He licked my clit fast and hard and then he forced three fingers in my ass. I screamed because of the pain the force caused. It had overwhelmed my pleasure, but only for a moment. Then I heard the door open to my bedroom.

As I turned to look, I saw Luis unleash another bite. He walked over and the one that was licking my pussy and finger fucking me in my ass looked up, paused, and told him, "Pain".

The second bite began to suck on my nipples and caress my belly and inner thighs around where the first bite was aggressively eating my pussy. My body shivered an orgasmic shake and the second bite kissed me passionately.

While I kissed him back, I grabbed the head of the first bite and I shoved it further into my pussy, holding him still on my g spot as I climaxed. My body poured into his mouth and I moaned a moan that was even foreign to myself. He ate right through my orgasm and I continued to cum in his mouth through it until I was exhausted.

He removed his fingers from my ass and his face from my pussy when he had taken all of the orgasm that my body had poured out. Bite 2 went into my bathroom and prepared my bath.

I was weak from exhaustion and it was easy for Bite 2 to lift me from my bed and take me to my bath. He bathed me and washed my hair again as Bite 1 kneeled beside my bath awaiting an order.

When I was clean to his satisfaction, he lifted me out of the bath and handed me to Bite 1 who was waiting with his arms open supporting a bath towel.

Bite 1 carried me to my bed and Bite 2 followed. They both wiped me dry as I laid on the bed lifeless. When I was dry, Bite 1 lifted me as Bite 2 placed my bathrobe on me and a pillow under my head. Then they both kneeled at my bedside awaiting orders.

I drifted off to sleep and I dreamt of Ro. The dreams were so realistic and I could feel him touching my body, licking my pussy, and making love to me. In one part of the dream when I was climaxing, I saw Reina in the corner and I woke up in fear.

Bite 1 and 2 were still there kneeled. I gave the order to eat my pussy again and he ate it until I came in his mouth. Bite 1 & 2 ate my pussy and fucked me, sometimes in my pussy and sometimes in my ass, several more times throughout the day.

I didn't feel like dealing with anything or anyone and stayed in my room being pleasured for the rest of the day.

When night time had come, I called for their pick up. But, I still didn't get out of bed. I was sick to my stomach and the only thing that gave me comfort was the pleasure that I felt from them.

Now that they were gone, it was all real again. My thoughts were interrupted by the sound of my cell phone ringing. It was Reina. What did this bitch want?!

"Hello" I answered. "I see you've been busy all day. What a fucking appetite, geez. You going to stay in the bed for the rest of the night?" Reina asked.

"Yea, I'm exhausted" I replied. "Well, ok, I'll come up and we can watch a movie" she said before hanging up.

Reina came up and put on a movie. We watched the movie in an awkward silence and she didn't try to force conversation. I stayed lying down and she sat on the foot of the extremely large bed.

Every now and then she would laugh out loud at the comedy from the movie. When she did laugh, I stared at the back of her head in disbelief. She was carrying on like everything was normal, like Ro wasn't missing, and like I didn't know that she had something to do with it.

Watching her increased the anxious feelings that I was experiencing and I wanted to kill her. I could either be afraid of her or teach her that I wasn't. I had to make a decision.

The plans had changed. I was going to find Ro and then kill Reina.

15 AN UNEXPECTED FRIENDSHIP

The next day I got up. It was a business as usual day for me. Reina and I had meeting with the Governors and we discussed territory growth, including the need to get rid of any un-cooperating competitors.

After the meeting I spent a couple hours in the library reviewing the books and ensuring the math was correct. I reviewed the books with the territory maps and took notice of debt collection books, something I had never considered doing before.

In the evening, I took my car and I rode down to the hood. I talked to several people who were considered to know everything moving, and many of our distros, trying to get a lead on anything I could concerning the whereabouts of Ro.

Nobody seemed to know anything about his disappearance. It was a weird type of silence as Ro was the high school football star and was known by everybody who was anybody. And, nobody was talking about him missing? That wasn't even some shit that made sense to me.

I was about to give up, but I decided to check one last resource, Candace.

She had been our neighbor and building manager for years and she was the nosiest Bitch in the hood. If it happened, she would surely know it. I was certain that her nosiness would get her killed one day.

I rode down to my old apartment and there she was, as always, sitting on the porch being a nosey bitch. While I was parking I could see her nosey ass watching my car.

I wasn't parked five minutes before she met me at my car. I let down the window and greeted her with a fake smile.

"Hi Candace", I said.

"Summer, girl you look as pretty as the first day I saw you. What you doing over here? Yo Mama ain't living over here no mo.", she replied to me.

"Well, a friend that I used to go to school with has gone missing and I was helping his parents search for him" I told her.

"You mean that same friend that you used to be parked in that car with doing god knows what when you were in high school?" she asked in a judging way.

I said in a very sarcastic voice, "Do you know anything about the missing boy or not Candace?"

"I ain't the one to be starting no rumors", she started. *Of fucking course you are.* "But I heard that the new guy around here had something to do with his disappearance and people are keeping it real hush hush. They talking about him getting rid of anybody that's caught minding his business." Candace told me in a frightened voice.

"New guy? What new guy?" I asked her.

"Summer, this ain't nothing you needing go involving yourself in. You done good for yourself, dun went off to college. Leave this hood shit alone. Let the police do their job" she said.

"Candace, please. He was my friend. I loved him and I have to find him", I replied. She looked around to check the surrounding and then she leaned over closer to my car window.

"The new guy, Black guy, well dressed. He always looking like he's a real estate agent but ain't never selling no property. He used to visit yo Mama when you were a little younger", she said.

She's talking about fucking TJ!

Before I could respond my cell phone rang. It was Reina. "Hello?" I answered.

"Reina, we need to talk, now. I'm being told that you're sticking your nose where it don't belong", she continued.

"What exactly do you mean Reina? And who are you being told by?" I asked in an irritated tone.

"Meet me back at the house, now!" she shouted into the phone and then disconnected.

I turned to Candace and explained that something came up and I needed to get back to school. She suspiciously waived me off and I sped off.

One thing was for certain, I was getting sick of this Bitch thinking she could tell me what to do and when to do it. And I must have been close to finding answers, because Rei was pretty pissed about my probing.

I was going to give her an ultimatum, either tell me what she did with Ro, or I'd figure it out myself by whatever means necessary.

I sped down the highway ignoring the changing neighborhoods along the drive. I was focused and pissed. Somehow, I didn't feel afraid of Reina anymore, revenge was my focus. I needed to find out what TJ had to do with it.

Getting to the Bottom of Things

I took a hard turn off the upcoming exit without even thinking about it and I headed back toward the direction I had just left.

I picked up my phone and dialed TJ. "Yo" he answered. "Let's meet, now. Where are you?" I replied.

"Summer, to what do I owe the pleasure?" he asked.

"Let me be clear, either we meet now or I'm shutting down the deal you've seemingly arranged with Reina" I told him in a very stern voice. "I'm not with the shits and I think you know exactly what I want" I said.

"I'm on the East End, meet me at the Fish Market in fifteen minutes. I certainly hope you're ready for the answers you're looking for', he said. I hung up on him and headed toward the Fish Market.

The Fish Market was a mutual territory for dealers. It was not uncommon to have meetings there because it was a rule amongst all of the organization that it was safe, neutral grounds. No one dared to break the treaty that was in place there, not even Reina.

When I arrived at the Fish Market I grabbed my pistol from my arm rest and put it in the back of my jeans. It was a habit and a lesson, we never took a meeting without being armed.

TJ was waiting for me outside of the Fish Market with one of his Distros. They greeted me with a handshake when I approached them.

I turned to his Distro and said, "This will be a private meeting, you may wait outside." He looked at TJ who nodded the approval as he held the door open for my entrance into the Fish Market.

When we walked in all of the employees disappeared to the back of the restaurant to allow TJ and I privacy.

"Where is Ro?!" I scolded TJ. I didn't take my eyes off him for a second as I was reading his body language. But, nothing about him said that he intended to lie.

"Summer, I think you know where Ro is and I think you know exactly why he's there" he responded very seriously. "You tried to play a very dangerous game with a very dangerous person and it cost a very expensive price."

"TJ, I don't know what you're talking about, enough with the fucking riddles. Just come out with it! I demanded of him.

He chuckled at me as if I had cracked some type of joke. "Summer, you know what your problem is?" he asked me rhetorically. "You're way too emotional and it's going to be the death of you" he finished.

"TJ, who are you? Really? I mean you just show up around here. It's clear you know my mother and at first you were totally against our organization. Now all of a sudden, you're Reina's pet?" I asked him.

"Don't you ever in your life disrespect me by calling me any bitch's pet", he said banging his fist on the table. He banged it so hard it knocked over all the table décor. "I'm a business man and any decision I make is beneficial to me!" he finished.

"So, are you going to tell me what happened to Ro or not?" I asked TJ aggravated at his ability to go around my questions.

"Your mother and I are old friends. That's what you should be asking questions about" he replied. "It seems to me that you're focused on the wrong shit."

I stood up to leave because he was clearly wasting my time. "Sit down. We're not done talking" he said.

"See, that's your problem", I told him. "You think you're always in control" I finished turning toward the exit of the diner.

"Summer, I want to help you, so does your mother", he replied, which caught my attention and I sat back down to hear what he had to say.

"Reina's family is no stranger to your mother. Her mother was a mistress of your grandfather's many years ago from the time your grandmother was pregnant with your mother until your mother started to become of age. From the moment she found out who you were she had plans for you. She's smart and she's dangerous. She is not to be fucked with in an amateur way", TJ said in a super serious tone.

"You wanna know why your mother went home? Because she felt it was the only way to save you. She would never go back there" TJ said before he stopped to see if I would respond.

But, I couldn't. I had so many questions. Save me from what? Reina knew Mama all these years? What plans had she had from me? Her mother was my Grandfather's mistress?! What in the entire fuck was going on?!

"What are you talking about? You're lying" I responded to TJ.

"Summer, now what do I gain from lying? Think about it. Do you think I would agree to meet you to discuss anything? My deal is done. You seriously think I was worried about Reina backing out of a deal on your word?" he asked.

He was right though. TJ was not the type of guy to be afraid and he had declined Reina's offer before. He was definitely a thorn in her side and he had nothing to gain by taking the meeting with me after he already had what he wanted.

"I'm listening", I said as I sat back. TJ began to explain everything.

"My brother was your mother's childhood sweetheart and they loved each other. They were together every day from the time they were five years old" he said as if he were remembering something.

"Your mother was always incredibly beautiful, even as a child, but her mother even more so. Everyone knew that your grandfather was always a lover of beautiful women and had many, even in your grandmother's younger days. He desired younger women. He cheated often, and they seemed younger and younger", he added.

"But there was one in particular that he could not get enough of, his own daughter. As your mother developed, she became more desirable to your Grandfather and he could no longer contain himself", TJ finished in a sad voice.

"The disgusting fucker started fucking his own daughter and it changed your mother. She became withdrawn from my brother and it broke his heart. He knew something was happening with her. Your Grandfather would no longer allow my brother to come around and forbid your mother from having any type of relationship with him. He knew that your mother was in love with my brother."

"When my brother confronted Maddy about it, she broke down and told him about the nights, and days, with her father. She begged my brother to save her from the torment of being raped by her father. She had no one to protect her, not even her own mother, who knew that it was happening and despised her daughter for being loved by your grandfather"

"My brother and your mother planned to run away together. On the night they were supposed to meet, he found a letter from Maddy that told him she couldn't run away with him. Your grandfather had impregnated her and she wanted to keep her family together. That night my brother hung himself" TJ said in a drawn off distant tone.

"Pregnant?" I asked TJ in a surprised tone. "Summer, your grandfather is your biological father. Your grandmother knows. He treated your mother like she was his fucking girlfriend, instead of his daughter. When she confessed to her mother that she was pregnant by her father, your grandmother disowned her and kicked her out" TJ finished.

I felt a stabbing pain as his words echoed in my ears. I knew most of it because Mama had told me, but she never told me who my father was and I was fucking disgusted to my stomach that I was the product of an incestuous rape.

TJ started again, "I've been checking up on your mother since she left. It's what my brother would have wanted. Sometimes I bring her letters that my brother wrote but never gave to her when your grandfather forbid them to see each other. It's the only time I get to see her eyes light up with life again"

"That's what I was doing at your apartment that day. I'm not really her dealer, but she didn't want you finding out about me and digging into your past. She always said you were smarter than I could ever imagine, and nosey too", he laughed.

"I looked into Reina after the day she pulled the strap on me, it was very hard finding out who she was which verified to me that she was hiding something. There was literally no record of Reina anywhere. It was apparent that she knew more about me than she was leading on. She was ready to pop me" TJ said in a suspicious tone.

That's when I found out that the organization that was trying to burn my business out of the hood for turning them down, belonged to this young girl.

How had a young girl who had never been heard of gained so much power? It was only one way; she had to come from an established power. The only type of families that powerful are political families and crime families, and there weren't many at the level that Reina held" TJ ended in anxiousness.

He leaned over to me and began to whisper, "Sydney, oh, my fault, you know her as Reina, had gone completely off the grid after her mother died, until her father came up missing and Reina appeared. It was said that Sydney went crazy and her father put her away. She was never heard from again. Now what's the odds of that? That bitch is Sydney and she is responsible for the disappearance of her own damn father" TJ said with a slight panic in his voice.

"I came back to find you and try to keep you from her. By the time I came back you were already gone. I told Maddie and she told me she had to go home. She had to save you" TJ said. When you called me to arrange the meeting, I thought I might get the time to talk to you, but it was apparent Reina had her hooves in you and your loyalty was uncanny", TJ said.

I sat up in my chair and he must have saw the look of panic on my face because he grabbed my hand. I didn't even realize that I was quivering.

"Let me get this straight, this bitch is a psychopath? And I'm living with her?!" I said as I began to freak out.

TJ grabbed my hands tighter, "Summer, calm down, you have to think. Stop being led by your emotions. It's going to get you killed!" he finished.

"I gotta get my shit, I gotta get out of there! She's expecting me! Oh my god, she called me and told me that she knew I was sticking my nose where it didn't belong!" I screamed.

"Summer, you cannot just leave! She will kill you!" TJ said.

"I don't care, I'm not staying one more day with this crazy bitch!" I replied.

"She will kill Maddy", TJ said, looking at me seriously. His words hit me like a ton of bricks and I felt like I was unable to move.

She will kill Mama.

TJ sat up straight and said, "She told me that she knew who I was and why I was at your mother's apartment. She also knew that I had been poking my nose where it didn't belong. She told me that you loved Ro and he was going to take you away from her so she seduced him and started fucking him. She didn't expect to fall in love with him, but she did."

"She knew you were at the door watching them and she knew you called her intentionally so that she could hear you fucking him. Since Ro couldn't stay away from you and she couldn't have him to herself, no one could" he said.

TJ continued, "She gave me a choice, I kill him, or she kills you", So, Ro is at the bottom of the lake in a box. "He's in the same place she put her father" he said casually.

An overwhelming feeling came over me and I could not hold it back. I began to cry. I sobbed for many reasons, not just because Reina, or Sydney, whoever the bitch was, had TJ kill Ro.

I cried because I had trusted her and I had been foolish enough to believe that Reina didn't know my intentions all along. I was the reason Ro was dead, because I started a very dangerous love triangle.

When I saw them together that night, I knew Reina loved him from the way she made love to him. She didn't fuck him how she fucked business. She gave me the chance to tell her I saw them because she had hopped I'd walk away from Ro, but I didn't. Instead I let emotions cloud my judgement.

And because of that, I paid a price. I had lost the only man I'd ever loved.

"What do I do TJ?" I said in a desperate tone.

"Summer, you are not weak. You are not an employee, she was foolish enough to make you a partner. You are the only one in a position to get close enough to her to solve your own problem" he responded.

I took a deep breath, and said, "You're right, I'm going to kill her."

TJ put his hand to his chin in deep thought and then said, "The only way to weaken her is to be honest with her, to a certain degree. You're going to have to tell her that you know she had something to do with the disappearance of Ro and that you're angry with her about it. But, you're going to have to maintain a level of normalcy. Let her teach you every aspect of the business. Confront her about her secrets and you being her best friend. Tell her you know she had an affair with Ro. You have to secure her trust. And then you do, then you will have the advantage."

"Your mother has returned home because your grandfather has just won another term as Governor He's in a very powerful positon and she plans to use that to give you a whole different level of advantage over Reina. I don't know how she will do it, and I don't even know if I want to know. But, there is one thing that Maddy is not good at, and that's failing" TJ said.

I checked my phone and I had more than thirty missed calls from Reina.

"I have to go", I told TJ. "I'll be in touch, please tell Mama that I love her and I'm thinking of her", I said as I got up and ran out of the Fish Market.

When I got in my car I called Reina back. "What do you want Reina?!"

"Summer, I told you to get here two hours ago and then you stop answering my calls?!" Reina said in a shitty tone.

"Reina, you don't tell me what to do! I'm your partner and not your child. Get some fucking self-control" I screamed at her.

She was silent. "I know you had an affair with Ro and I know you're the reason why he's missing. I'm supposed to be your fucking best friend but you're turning out to be like a goddamn priest, you get everything from me and give me nothing in return" I scolded her.

"Summer", Reina, Sydney, or whoever the fuck she was started. "Don't fucking open your mouth unless the truth is coming out of it" I said in a threatening tone.

"I think its best we talk about it, in person" Reina said. "Can you come to the house? I can explain everything."

"Fine, I'm on my way." "And Rei, no bullshit ok? I'm not in the fucking mood" I said before I hung up.

I drove 90 mph across the freeway heading home. My adrenaline was pumping times two. It would have made sense for me to be scared. Instead, I was angry and I wanted to kill this Bitch. I could not believe what she did to Ro, but then again, I didn't know here very well at all.

When I pulled up to the house I threw the car in park and hopped out. I stormed in the front door and slammed it hard enough to come off the hinges.

It must have gotten Reina's attention because she came to meet me rapidly. I could tell from her facial expressions she was not happy, but I really didn't give a fuck!

"What the fuck did you do to Ro?" I screamed. She looked at me in her snobby ass composed look at turned to walk toward the library.

On her walk over she turned back to me and said, "Summer, lower your voice" casually. I followed her into the library and she took a seat on the sofa where it looked like she had been having a cup of tea.

I stood across the room at the door glaring at her with every bit of hatred I felt coursing through my veins. She didn't seemed affected by it at all.

"You're asking me what I did to Ro. You should ask yourself what *you* did to Ro" Reina said in a sarcastic voice.

"Reina, what the fuck is that supposed to mean?!" I spat out.

"It means exactly what I said. Ro paid the price for playing a dangerous game. It's the nature of the business Summer, you know that."

"Reina, he was not business and you fucking know it!" I screamed at her, furious that she would compare the two.

"On the contrary, the minute he decided he could fuck me, tell me he loved me and not mean it, he became business. He was supposed to go to that meeting to tell you that we were going to be together."

"You did this to Ro, you determined his fate the minute you dialed my number Summer. You had a chance to walk away, the night you saw us together. He had a chance to tell you we were together, but he didn't. He paid the price.

"I am the one mourning here. I had to choose between two people that I loved. I chose you Summer" Reina snapped at me. "And because of your transgressions I had to retire him" she finished sadly.

I looked at Reina in horror. I knew she had did it, but hearing her say it made the monster that she was real. I felt a crushing feeling inside and it must have shown.

"Oh, cheer up Summer. There will be other men. He is not the first man that I've loved that I 've had to retire" she said as she chuckled.

She looked exactly like the devil, if it existed. This Bitch was seriously crazy.

"I'm going to bed" I told her as I turned to leave the library.

"Ok, goodnight Summer" the crazy bitch said as I was heading out the door.

"Oh, Summer?" Reina called out for me to turn around.

"If you so much as think about leaving here, backing out the business. Maddy is dead" she said as picked up her cup of tea.

I stormed out of the library in a panic. *She will kill Mama if I leave!*

The truth was, I didn't know if she would kill Mama if I didn't leave. It was evident that she was unpredictable.

I ran up to my room. When I got to the door, I broke down in tears again.

Get your shit together Summer, you can't win like this! I told myself. It was so hard not to be overwhelmed with emotions and to not feel defeated but I had to think of a plan. Reina, Sydney, was a fucking coo coo nest.

I went to the desk by my bed to find the card that had the number to reach Mama. When I opened the desk drawer, it was empty. There were no papers at all. I looked in the second drawer, then the third. Nothing.

I quickly charged to my closet to find my purses and looked through the purse I wore the night I called it. It wasn't there. The card was, gone.

I stormed back into my bedroom and fell on the bed in anger. As I was lying on my bed trying to think, I saw it in the clock on the bedroom wall. It was a blinking red light. It was super small, unnoticeable if the room would have been lighted.

Why would the clock have a blinking red light?

I grabbed my cell phone to text TJ.

Camera in room, been watching me

I picked up the desk phone, "Connect me to Reina. She picked up on the first ring.

"Summer, what's wrong now?"

"Rei, you put cameras in my room?" I asked in a fake disappointed tone.

"Well Summer, you've been acting weird lately. You're disappearing and not answering your phone" she said.

"So, you invade my privacy in OUR house. You're acting like I'm a guest" I replied.

"You are right, and I'm sorry. I didn't know if I could trust you. But it's obvious, you were just angry and you're completely yourself. I'll have them removed tomorrow, k?" she said.

"Fine. And if you want us to remain best friends, perhaps you should be a better one" I told her in a fake sad tone.

"Sum, I'm, I'm sorry. You're right. Let's have breakfast in the morning."

"Ok, I love you" I replied.

"I love you too" she said happily before she hung up.

16 AND IT BEGINS

I woke up the next morning at 6am, got showered, dressed and headed downstairs. Reina was already having breakfast.

I walked up to her, kissed her on the cheek and sat down next to her. I grabbed some food off the platter and began to eat. I created casual conversation and then told her I was heading out to check on the parlors. She started to give me a look of suspicion but immediately corrected it.

I hopped in my car and headed for the hood. About twenty five minutes into the drive I pulled off the freeway and into a nearby gas station. The neighborhood was the most decent that I would find that close to the hood so it had to do.

I parked, went into the gas station to get some change and back outside to use the pay phone.

"TJ, its Summer. I'm at the gas station off the 43, can you pick me up? Don't call my cell phone. Bring me a burner with you."

Then, I waited. It was about thirty minutes before TJ arrived. When he did, he had a burner phone in hand.

"Summer, what's up?" he asked me. "My car is a gift from Reina and I don't know what she's capable of. I needed a way to get around and you were the only person I could think of to help me."

"Of course, anything you need" he replied.

"Do you know where Sydney was institutionalized at?" I asked him. He thought for a moment.

"No, I don't. But, your mom would" he said.

He picked up the phone to call my mother. My heart skipped a beat. "Don't tell her I'm with you" I said quickly.

"Why? She would want to talk to you Summer" he said.

"Please TJ. She will kill my mother. She told me. I don't want to involve Mama any more than we've already done. From here on out, it has to be just you and me" I told him.

He shook his head and dialed Mama. "Madeline please. "Tyson Jordan", he said after a few minutes.

I heard her voice through his phone the minute she spoke and my eyes filled with tears. She sounded exactly the way I remembered her.

TJ asked her about Sydney and where she had been institutionalized. Mama asked about me and he assured her that I was fine and that I didn't know anything about what was going on. The ironic thing that was happening was the fact that Mama wanted to protect me as bad as I wanted to protect her.

I could hear Mama talking to TJ but I couldn't hear what she was saying clearly. TJ was silent as he listened intently without looking up at me.

I stared at his so hard that I thought I'd burn a hole into the side of his face. I was anxious to know what he and Mama were talking about. He spent almost 15 minutes listening to Mama before responding, "Ok" and hanging up.

"Well, what did she say?" I asked anxiously. "She gave me the hospital where Sydney was institutionalized. We can head there now."

"And?" I asked. He looked at me confused. "And, what?" he said.

"What else did she say?" I asked him annoyed at his delay in answering my question.

"It's nothing to concern yourself with right now" he said as he drove toward the expressway heading back the direction that I lived.

We drove for what seemed like forever. He asked me many questions about Reina and her behavior and made me repeat details of how she looked, or what she said when I told her I knew about Ro. I assured him that he had not been a part of the conversation and that Reina had no idea that I ever talked to him.

He reminded me to be careful and watch my back. He also commended me on ditching the car and getting a burner, saying that it was a well-played move but I'd have to go much further to fool Sydney.

After about two hours, we reached the mental health complex where Reina had grown up. This place looked like Beverly Hills. The front doors looked like they belonged on a white house.

TJ and I got out of the car and headed toward the door. Today was one of them days where I was happy Reina required business attire. It would make it much easier to get information dressed in business attire than any sort of casual wear, even very expensive casual wear.

As we approached the door, a teenage girl met us. She was tall, slender build with long blonde hair. She was neatly dressed in a dark blue Dolce and Gabbana jumpsuit.

"Hi!" she said happily.

"Hello" I said, attempting to go around her, but she blocked our entrance to the door.

"Excuse me" I said, annoyed at her childish ass behavior.

"Hi!" she responded, as if what I was saying didn't matter.

"Hello, can you show us in?" TJ asked the girl in a voice that sounded like he was speaking to a 6 year old.

"Yes!' she said happily, and opened the door to let us into the building.

The marble floors caught my attention. They were so shiny. None of the staff was dressed in normal mental health attire, instead, they were all dressed in suits and ties or neatly tucked high end fabrics.

The girl dropped us off at the reception desk.

"Can I help you?" she asked.

"Yes, I was hoping you could help me. I'm trying to find my sister" I told the receptionist.

"This is a private facility, we don't give out information on patients" the receptionist lady responded.

TJ stepped in front of me. "Of course not, how foolish of us. We will tell Senator Gates that we were unsuccessful, have a good day" he said and turned away.

"Wait!" the receptionist yelled. "I didn't know you were from Salvador Gates' office. Is there anyone that I can call to confirm?"

"Of course" TJ said and he gave the receptionist a number. "You can ask for

Madelyn Gates, I hope she isn't annoyed with having to handle these shenanigans as she is very busy. This is her daughter Summer."

A look of nervousness and embarrassment covered the receptionist's face.

"No, that won't be necessary. I didn't know it was a Gates that you were looking for" she said.

"Actually, she's not a Gates" TJ said trying to be more discreet. "It's a matter our family would like to keep private" he finished in a hush tone.

"Ah, I see, what is the name?" she asked.

"Sydney Jordan" TJ told the receptionist.

I feel like I just heard that last name somewhere. I thought to myself. It was almost as if it were deja vu. I stood and waited as the receptionist typed the name into the computer. After several minutes a look of fear covered her face.

"She is someone that your family does not want to know. I hope you all know what you're doing! She is no longer at this facility. She disappeared a few years ago after stabbing her psychiatrist to death" the receptionist said in a grave tone.

TJ and I looked at each other with a look of fear that could not even be described in a horror film.

"Excuse me?" I said, looking at the receptionist as if she'd made a mistake.

"She has a pattern of violence. According to her file, she had several altercations with the other patients, one which resulted in her a young girl losing her right eye. As a result, the psychiatrist had her confined to solitary for several weeks.

When her time was up she acted completely normal and then later that day, during group, she stabbed him with a pair of meat cutters. It was said that she stole them from the kitchen after throwing scolding hot water on the cook."

What in the entire fuck? Psycho is an understatement, this was some Exorcist type shit!

TJ and I just stood quietly, listening to the many other horror stories that the receptionist read off. She concluded by telling us that she was confined to solitary indefinitely with one hour of recreation outside alone a week. One day she was taken out for recreation and when the staff went to retrieve her, she was gone. The gates were still locked and they had no idea how she got out. She had not been seen or heard from again.

"Her next of kin is listed as", the receptionist started.

"That will be all, thank you", TJ interrupted and grabbed me to pull me out the door quickly.

"Wait!" I said as he was ushering me into the car, "Maybe we can find out more information by reaching out to the next of kin" flustered that he had interrupted the receptionist right when we were getting somewhere.

"It's not necessary, she's dangerous and I think you should fall back for your sake" he said.

"I don't have a choice, I have to do this. How long do you think it will be before she decides I'm expendable? Or that she can't trust me? She will kill me, and if not me, she will kill Mama!' I screamed at him.

TJ was quiet as he started up the car. "You're right. She will eventually decide you're no longer necessary for whatever plan she's trying to accomplish. I have to talk to Maddy. She can help me figure out what to do next. Summer, don't do anything until I say so" TJ warned me.

"I don't want Mama involved!" I replied. "She's already involved, and when the time is right, you'll understand everything."

I looked at TJ. I had no idea what he meant about how Mama was involved and why he was giving me shit about coming out with everything. But, I didn't have time to deal with that at the time. I was scared shitless.

I had to continue living as normal with a complete fucking psycho who could tell when I was lying and was already suspicious of me. At any given time she could snap. She would make me disappear just like Ro and her father and nobody would even miss me except maybe TJ. Even then, he would probably be next.

I didn't even know how deep it ran. Did Luis know about Sydney? What about the distros and the Governors'? Were they all in on it? Would they be the ones to do it? I knew Reina, Sydney, would more than likely not going to get her hands dirty. She seemed to keep a low profile. The worst part of it was that no one ever saw it coming.

Suddenly, I trouble breathing and the houses that we were passing began to become blurred. I grabbed for the window button in an attempt to let it down. I just needed some air, but I couldn't do it.

My chest began to close in on me and I could hear TJ calling out for me, but it sounded as if I was beneath water. I was struggling to breathe, I was afraid. I remembered having this feeling before, but I couldn't remember when. I knew it was when I was younger and I knew what it was. Panic attack. I was experiencing a panic attack.

I spilled out the words as blurred as someone who was inebriated, "Pull over."

TJ quickly took the next sharp turn into an empty warehouse parking lot and threw the car into park. He was clearly panicking about my breathing.

I grabbed his hand and slid it up my skirt opening the side of my panties so his finger could glide in and I left it on my pussy. He looked at me with hesitation and I pushed my body down on the seat to force his finger to meet my clit. He started to finger me and my breathing began to regulate.

I moaned softly and it turned him on. He leaned over to nibble my ear lobe as he fingered me softly. I grabbed his hand to give it a slight push further into my pussy.

He reached over me with his free hand and reclined my seat so it was laid completely on the back seat. He removed his finger from my pussy and pulled my panties down. He looked at me.

"Fuck me" I said softly.

He leaned back and unzipped his pants, opened the opening to his boxers, and pulled his dick out. It was already rock hard and I was pleased at the appearance.

He climbed over the arm rest and in between my legs. He raised one of my legs to the dash and the other to the tip of the steering wheel and he stuck his dick in my pussy, raw.

It was the first time in my life I had ever felt a dick in me without the use of a condom and it felt very different. I had not known a pleasure like this and apparently neither did he.

When he stuck his dick in me he groaned in excitement and pleasure and he kissed me in my mouth with such passion.

He grabbed the top of my seat with one hand and lifted my bottom with the other hand so that I was slightly tilted in the air.

I sounded in pain as I felt the full length of his dick and it felt like he was in my uterus. He didn't even flinch, it was if he didn't hear me.

He fucked my pussy slowly and steady and he kissed me passionately. I moaned and she wet up even more. He could feel my excitement and it drove him wild. He moaned so tenderly and called out my name.

My excitement overtook me and I pushed him out of me. I turned him over in the tight space and I sat on his dick which stood upright. The space was tight but I didn't take notice to it. I was caught up in the immense pleasure I was experiencing from the feel of his bare dick inside of me.

Even with the lean of my body from being in the seat, I still groaned with a mixture of pain and pleasure. I felt every part of him and I rode him slowly.

I clasped my belly muscles causing my pussy to lock on him and I rode him back and forth. My pussy held on so tight that I moaned in an excitement that was even foreign to myself.

He pulled out one of my titties and he sucked it softly, caressing it while I swayed every muscle in my pussy on top of him. And then, there was a feeling. I knew it was orgasmic, but I had never in my life felt it quite like this.

I looked at TJ, who I could tell felt it too, and he could barely let a sound come out. I didn't change any position and the feeling was timeless. It was as if time stopped for several minutes. Neither of us could even moan with the pleasure that this feeling brought.

And after holding it as long as we could, we both let out a moan in sync and I felt him fill me up. I let my energy flow from deep inside the walls of my pussy and I poured out all over him as he filled me up.

And then I collapsed onto him, weak. We laid there for several minutes, in the car, wet from the extreme passion we gave each other, silent.

Finally, I lifted up so he could climb back over to the driver's seat, and I put my panties back on. We didn't say a word and he drove me back to my car in complete silence. It wasn't regret that I felt from him, it was more like fear of anyone finding out what we'd done.

Once we got back to my car, I got out TJ's car without saying goodbye. He waited as I got into my car before pulling off. I sat in my car for just a moment replaying the extreme pleasure I had just enjoyed.

I checked my phone and saw that Reina had called several times and picked the phone up to return her call. Before I could dial her back to return her call, she was calling again.

"Hello?!" I answered in my usual annoyed voice when she called me repeatedly.

"Summer, where are you?" Reina asked.

"I'm in route to the house, why? What's up?" I replied.

"Nothing, I've been calling you and you didn't answer. I guess I just..." she said, drifting off in an uneasy voice.

"You thought what?" I asked in a surprising, yet accusatory tone. She was silent.

"Well, never mind. You want to catch lunch?" she asked.

"Sure" I said, with my stomach turning at the thought of having to eat lunch with a fucking psycho. "I'm in route to the house, I'll see you in a minute."

I drove back to the house, my mind spinning, trying to practice hiding the fear. It was if I felt like she'd be able to look at me and tell and I knew if Reina found out that I knew who she really was, she would not hesitate to kill me. It was not going to be one of those beg for forgiveness things; she would show no mercy.

I picked the phone up to text TJ. I wanted him to know where I was heading, in case she already knew what was up and really planned to kill me. I wasn't certain he'd be able to do anything about it, but at least he could tell Mama.

Although I was scared, I drove toward the house. I knew that I had to carry out my plan. It was kill Reina or be killed; not just me, but Mama would be killed too. She would likely torture me by making me watch her slaughter Mama and then kill me. Reina was evil like that.

When I made it to the house Rei was waiting for me on the porch and ushered me in the house excitedly. When I walked through the door, Luis was waiting with a Chanel box. She took the box from Luis's hand and gave it to me.

I opened the box and it was the most beautiful Camelia Bracelet made by Chanel. The bracelet was about $15,000 and the surprised expression showed over my face.

I could tell from her face that she was pleased with my expression and she removed the bracelet from the box and put it on my arm.

I could not find the words to say. I stood there in complete paralysis to see such a beautiful piece and to know that a goddamn psycho had gifted it to me. "Thank you Rei", I said and hugged her.

She took my hand and led me to the kitchen where a massive spread of food covered the table.

"Wow, Reina, what is this? What is the occasion?" I asked surprised by all of the food. She was acting as if we were having some sort of party.

"Summer! It's a celebration!" she said in a weird, scary way.

"What are we celebrating?" I asked, baffled at what the psycho bitch was talking about.

"You will see, in due time. Let's eat!" she said and pulled out a chair for me to sit down.

We ate and she chattered away like a high school girl. She made jokes and she laughed so hard at them herself that she didn't even notice that I wasn't enjoying the joke as much as she. For the first time she chatted more than she listened.

I could not understand why the hell Reina, or Sydney, was so damn happy, but it made it a lot easier to tolerate her.

We enjoyed the lunch and then went out back for a swim. The day seemed like the early days when I first moved in, before any of the madness ever started. As long as things were like that, the plan would be easy to carry out. It meant Reina trusted me and that is what I needed from her in order to succeed.

17 SURPRISES

It had become easier to accept, the fact that I would have to go on living as if I knew nothing until the time came to act. Reina was so pleasant so it made it easy. It was actually the first time in a long time that I felt safe with her.

She loosened her grip on me and I could see the untrusting vibe leave her. I was able to come and go as I pleased and she didn't call me often. It was if everything had returned to normal.

A month had gone by and I had started to fuck TJ regularly. I enjoyed feeling him inside of me bare. I felt every stroke and his sizable dick was pleasing to the inside of my walls.

Every day I left the house, before heading down to take care of business, I met him. He would eat my pussy in the car until I came on his face, he would eat it in the bathroom at a restaurant, and he would eat it at his spot. He fucked me so good and we orgasmed together every time.

When we went a couple days without seeing each other we'd practically be feigning for each other like coke heads.

He stick his dick in bare sometimes tearing my panties because in a hurry to feel me before he exploded from excitement. When I saw that my pussy brought him to his peak, I'd push him out of me and make him stick his dick in my mouth.

I'd suck his dick and lick his balls as if I had just tasted a Popsicle for the first time. He'd grab my hair and pull hit forcefully, but not enough to hurt me, forcing his dick into my throat sometimes enough for me to have a gag reflex.

I could feel every stroke that his bare dick put in, which was much better than the sex I was served at the Tables. Even though I still had snacks, often in the house, was served at the parlors, and was even fucking one of the Governors-Black, none felt as good as TJ's.

He had me alone and he had me with Trice. Trice and I had each other together and we had him together. Sometimes we had each other first and when we had pleased each other while he watched, we invited TJ to join.

Trice would show up whenever I called and do whatever I asked of her. She was so sweet and shy. But, she came to life when it was time for her to make me

103

happy.

She knew exactly how I liked my pussy licked. She would lick it so soft and suck on my clit softly, careful enough to read my body language.

Trice loved my titties and I loved hers. I would suck her titties, sometimes, for several minutes, while I just fingered her.

I loved to kiss her. Her lips were so full and her freakiness always aroused me.

Somedays I'd bring my dildo along and fuck her with it while I sucked her pussy until she came. Other days, I'd make TJ fuck her while I kissed her and sucked her titties.

Most times TJ fucked me and I ate he pussy until he came. And then, she'd eat my pussy until I came and we woiuld lay down together and just stare at one another.

Trice would tell me how beautiful I was and how lucky TJ was to have me. TJ would listen, sometimes, he would eat Trice's pussy while I laid next to her starting at her, becoming aroused by her moans, until I was turned over to open my legs.

The minute I turned over, they would both come to please me. They were both very attentive to me and were always aiming to ensure I left the most pleased.

TJ and Trice made me happy. I was intrigued by the different ways TJ would fuck me and I loved how he would fuck me no matter where we were.

Trice was the same. She took enjoyment in pleasing me and she ate my pussy better than even TJ could.

I loved his aggressiveness and his freakiness. I loved that he loved to have me with Trice and enjoyed watching us please each other.

He would bend me over the car in the parking lot in broad daylight and he would fuck me hard, pulling my hair and grabbing my waist, from the pleasure my pussy caused him, so hard that it would leave bruises.

He kissed me as if his life depended on it and I knew from the way he looked at me that he was in love with me.

TJ reminded me of Ro which made me sad and because of that I couldn't fall in love with him. But, I was satisfied with him and I wanted to one day make our relationship exclusive.

For the time being, business went on as usual. I took care of the territories outside of fun and I learned everything I could about the business.

I secured Reina's trust and she opened up to me about things she had never shared with me. I learned about the Black Book, which listed every political customer that ever had a reservation at any of The Tables.

I learned about our debt holders, off shore accounts, safe houses, and inside Federal agents that kept us off the radar.

I carried myself differently. I was more serious and never dressed down like I had done in the past. I acted as a partner and I made decisions without Reina's permission. She didn't contest it, instead she backed the decisions and even referred decisions to me about the business. It was as if I was turning into Reina. I was taking over the business and she seemed content.

Poisoned

Reina and I had a meeting with the Governors about expanding into a new territory scheduled for the end of the week so I had to compose the setup and decide which building we would choose for the clinic and where we would open the new Table in the territory. Anytime we expanded it was always a very busy time.

I knew that whoever currently owned that territory wouldn't go easy, they never did. I was the first point of contact and my approach was always though dinner and snacks. In the past I had joined often, but lately, not so much. I only sampled the snacks and meals, as did Reina and usually once they were in rotation, they only really saw me in passing. It was a big change from the past. I had embraced my new position and I had become as ruthless as Reina.

I was losing who I was and I had lost sight of the plan. The feeling of power was more than the need for revenge and TJ didn't attempt to even keep me grounded in the plan. Instead, he encouraged my take over. It all felt right- him, Trice, my position, MY BUSINESS.

The day of the meeting, I woke up early like I had been doing for the past six weeks. It was one of the things that Reina did. She was always up before 6am and I had picked up that trait.

I got showered, dressed, and down to the kitchen by 7am where Reina was already seated at the table slid down in her seat, having her pussy aggressively licked by a new menu item.

She opened her eyes to acknowledge my entrance and I sat down to be served breakfast by the wait staff. I started to go over the numbers of the territory while I was having a cup of the juice that was waiting for me, and paused long enough for her to let out a moan of pleasure and release from the clear excitement she had experienced.

When Reina was done and had been cleaned up, I continued.

Suddenly, I felt dizzy and I began to sweat. I leaned over the chair and I began to vomit aggressively. I could see Reina from the chair, watching me without moving.

She poisoned me! I thought to myself as I grabbed at the table cloth in an attempt to get up from the table.

I could hear Reina laughing. I looked over at her with a look of fear in my eyes, but she just sat right there and continued to eat.

The wait staff was about to attempt to help me and Reina waved her hand causing them all to return to their standing position.

"Summer, sit down. Where are you trying to go?" she asked.

I sat back down in the chair, continuing to vomit, and prepared myself to die.

After what seemed forever, I stopped vomiting and was able to sit up. The wait staff immediately got cleaning utensils to clean up the puke that I had now spilled out on the table and the floor around my entire area.

"Did you fucking try to poison me?!" I asked her furiously.

"Summer, why on earth would you think that I would try to poison you?" she asked calmly.

"I don't know, you fucking tell me" I screamed at her with the slight energy that I had left.

All of the vomiting had made me exhausted. I was weak and dizzy and the reality was if she wanted to get out of the chair and drag me across the floor she could have, and there would be nothing that I could do.

"You look terrible Summer, why don't you go lie down and I'll take care of the meeting today" Reina said happily.

She motioned for Luis and Luis motioned for one of the new courses who picked me up from the table and carried me to my room.

He undressed me to my bra and panties before tucking me under the covers where I fell quickly to sleep.

I was awaken by the ringing of my cell phone on the desk next to my bed.

I had never seen the number before. "Hello?" I said sleepily.

"Summer, it's good to hear your voice. I have missed you so much". The voice hit me like a ton of bricks and my heart stopped for several seconds.

"Mama?" I replied, shocked to hear her voice.

"Yes, baby. It's me. I need to see you right away. Listen, you can't tell anybody. You can't trust anybody. Can you get out now?" she asked.

I could tell Mama was scared and that made me scared.

"Yes, I'll get dressed. Where do you want to meet?"

Mama gave me the address to meet and I jumped up from the bed to get dressed. As soon as I jumped up, the feeling hit me again and I ran to the bathroom to vomit.

After about tem minutes of vomiting, I was able to get cleaned and dressed. As soon as I was dressed I slipped out the bedroom door.

The house was quiet and it was dark. I had no idea that I had slept so long, but whatever poison Reina had used on me hadn't killed me and I was grateful.

I was still feeling very weak but I pushed myself out the front door and around to my car. I hopped in it, put the address in my phone's GPS, and drove off to meet Mama.

When I pulled up to the address, it was an abandoned warehouse. It looked like it had been in a fire. When I pulled into the lot, the doors opened and a gentlemen that must have been some sort of driver motioned me to pull inside of the garage like doors.

As I pulled in, I saw a limo parked off to the side, and there she was, as beautiful as I remembered, standing on the side of the limo waiting for me to park.

My eyes filled with tears and I was unable to contain them. I began to cry uncontrollably as I parked.

Mama met me at the door and as soon as I shut off the engine she opened my door and I could see the tears in her eyes. She embraced me quickly as I stepped out.

We hugged each other tightly for several minutes without even saying a word.

Finally we let go of each other and I could see the very worried look on Mama. She looked younger and I could tell she was clean.

"Mama, you look good" I said.

"Summer, you look sick. Are you ok?" she asked sadly.

"I think I've been poisoned. I've been vomiting nonstop and nauseous since the day I had breakfast with the psycho bitch Reina. I damn near passed out. I've been weak and unable to regain my strength."

Mama looked at me in great concern and I could tell she was more worried than I had ever seen her.

I had so many questions for Mama and I was prepared to ask them, but before I could, she interrupted me.

"Summer, you have to be careful. I recently found out some devastating news and I've been so worried about you. This news of poison worries me as I fear that I may be too late."

"Mama, what is it?!" I asked, curious about what could be more devastating than what she and TJ knew.

"Well, in order for me to tell you, I guess I have to tell you everything", Mama said sadly.

"Mama, tell me, it couldn't get worst that what it already is! TJ already told me that you know about Reina" I said matter of factly.

"TJ?" Mama asked in a weirdly clueless voice.

"Yes, TJ. He already told me that his brother was in love with you when you were teenagers and his brother committed suicide because he couldn't be with you".

Mama turned to me and looked at me with a grave look. "Summer, that muthafucka is lying" she said.

"I'm assuming this "TJ" that you're referring to is Tyson Jordan and he is not who he pretends to be!"

The words rang in my ear repeatedly!

18 TYSON JORDAN/HARU

"Summer, come, sit down" Mama said as she took my hand and let me to work bench on the side of the warehouse. I was quite relieved because I was really feeling weak.

"I am so sorry, about everything. I have kept you in the dark for so long and I fear that this is the reason that everything is happening."

Mama had my full attention. *What had she been keeping me in the dark about? How could she be responsible for any of it?*

I decided it was better not to ask questions, but to listen.

"Summer, remember I told you the story of my father's intimate activities with me. Well there was more to the story that I left out for a reason. I didn't want to hurt you" she said with her eyes planted on the ground.

"Mama, I know, TJ told me that your father, my grandfather, impregnated you with me" I replied, not even thinking.

"Summer, don't believe anything Tyson tells you. He's a manipulative liar and everything he does has a motive!" she said.

"I'm confused Mama, he said that he's been working with you to protect me from Reina.

"Who?" Mama asked in a strong, concerned voice.

"Reina, you know! The girl that I was best friends with and moved out with" I told her with a worried tone.

"Summer, I literally have no idea who this girl is or what you're talking about" she replied.

"Mama, I watched him call you and talk to you several times. I heard your voice!" I shouted at her.

"Summer, let me explain and I everything might help us make sense of this all.

"Summer, let me start with what Tyson told you. Tyson was adopted into the Jordan's family. They had already had another son, Sidnea Jordan Jr, and the child birth had damaged Mrs. Jordan's body. She was unable to have any more kids. They wanted to expand their family, so they adopted Tyson."

"I was going through a lot, being molested by my own father and I was unable to find attachment in any of the boys my age. Summer, you have to understand, my youth had been taken from me. I was forced to become a woman and I didn't want to be one" Mama said sadly.

"I couldn't love Sidnea the way that he loved me, my innocence was lost. I tried, I really did. I was so promiscuous. I was crying out for help. It's no excuse for what I've done."

"One day, when I was leaving a visit with Sidnea, I saw his father sitting in his study and I went in and seduced him. That was the beginning of an affair between us."

"Summer, I wasn't pregnant by my father, I was pregnant by Sidnea Jordan, and when Sid found out about it he committed suicide. The loss of her son drove Ms. Jordan crazy."

"Sidnea kept in touch with me and put me up until I had the baby. I gave birth to a beautiful girl that looked so much like Sid that it hurt to look at her. I called Sidnea and told him that I felt that he could care for our child better than I could. By that time he had told his wife of the affair and she welcomed the baby as her own. From the little I know, it healed her."

"Mama, what was that baby's name?!" I asked, almost scared to get the answer.

"Her name was Sydney, Sydney Gates" Mama said.

Holy shit! Sydney/Reina, the psychotic bitch is my sister!

Mama could tell from the look in my eyes that I was shocked.

"Summer, there is more. Before my father started fucking me he had many affairs. My mother knew of his affairs and she did everything she could to make herself more beautiful. She started focusing on her appearance more than the affairs."

"During that time she fell in love with her personal trainer, a Japanese man named Haru. It was the happiest I had ever seen my mother. She used to tell me that his name meant sunlight, and that is what he brought her, and peace."

111

"Wait, so you have a sister?" I asked, excited for Mama.

"Yes, I do Summer, but it is not what you think" she replied.

I was so confused. What else was there to think? Mama had a sister and I had an aunt!

"What do you mean Mama? Where is she?"

Mama looked at me sadly, "Summer, it is you. I am not your mother. I am your sister."

What in the entire fuck was Mama talking about?!

"When Mama found out she was pregnant she going to abort the pregnancy. She couldn't do it and she knew that she couldn't tell Haru that she was pregnant. He would want her to leave my father who was her sole source of support and marry him. She had become used to a certain type of lifestyle and she didn't want to give that up."

"She told my father that she was pregnant, thinking that it was an opportunity to save her marriage, to stop his affairs, but by that time he was already fucking me."

"A few years after I left, I was living in that shitty ass apartment building where I raised you and my mother showed up at my door, with you. You were only two years old. My mother was weeping, it was the first time I had seen any real emotion from her."

"She told me that my father's desire for beauty continued to get younger and she saw the same look in his eyes for you, that she had seen for me. She could not bear to let you endure what she had failed to protect me from. She left you there, with me, practically a kid that had no idea how to take care of a baby. I had given up my own damn baby."

"But, I could not bear to let my father do the things to you that he had done to me. There was so much guilt and sorrow from giving up Sydney too. So, I kept you and raised you as my own."

She began to weep as she continued, "One day my father, Salvatore Gates, showed up at our apartment to tell me that my mother was terminally ill and that her request was to have be brought home."

"I waited for you to come back. The letter you left said that you would come back for me, but you never did. I couldn't wait any longer, Mother was dying, so I went home."

"She wanted me to bring you to her. Mother wanted to tell you the truth."

"We hired a private investigator to find you, and that is when I found out that my biological daughter, Sydney, had done some very bad things and that she had you, along with Tyson."

"I went to Tyson to convince him to tell me where you were, or how to get to you and he told me that I had ruined his life by taking his best friend, Sidnea Jr., and that he would ruin my life by taking the only person that I ever loved, you."

"I warned him that Sydney was dangerous and that she would kill you and when she was done with him, she would kill him too, but he wouldn't listen."

I had the PI put a tail on Tyson's car and he followed you and him to the mental health complex where Sydney used to be committed."

I started to feel a shortness of breath mixed with anger. It was too much. Maddy had lied to me for years. My entire life had been fucked up again, but this time not by Reina. I didn't know who I was anymore. I tried to stand and then I fainted.

What's next?

"Summer? Summer?" I came to hear Maddy calling my name, with a look of panic and fear in her eyes. I sat up and looked at her as if I was looking at an alien for the first time.

I must have been out for several minutes because I could tell that she was completely freaked out and seconds away from calling the ambulance.

"You have lied to me my entire life. Everyone has lied to me my entire life. I have no idea who I am or where I come from. How could you?" I asked through tears.

"Summer, I am so sorry, for everything. I know sorry can't fix it, but I had to save you. I wanted you to have a life where you were in control of your body, something that I never felt. Part of me knew that someday we would have to have this conversation and I've been dreading it ever since."

"I know that you're angry and I wish we had time to give you time, but we don't. Sydney is dangerous. She knows who you really are and she wants to hurt me. She came at a time when I couldn't know love because everyone that ever used that word hurt me."

"The PI told me that he believed there was a tap on your phone which is why you can't go back. She will know that you've talked to me and she will tell Tyson. Summer, I'm afraid they will hurt you or worst. You have to come home with me."

"I can't" I said, "they will kill you, TJ told me that Reina will kill you, or Sydney, whoever she is. And, now that I know that he is in on it, I know they will" I told Maddy firmly.

"They've been playing me, but so have you. Everyone has made a fool of me. I've been so stupid, but I want what's mine and I plan on taking it!" I told Madelyn in Reina's tone.

"Summer, please, you're playing a dangerous game" she begged.

"Madelyn, I've been played enough and it's clear that everyone has me all the way fucked up. I'm taking what's mine. Reina and TJ will pay for what they've done, you just watch. I have to go, but I'll be in touch. Take care of yourself" I told her before hugging her and heading toward my car.

Maddy had just changed my life. I didn't even have time to process it because I was angry. I was angry that TJ and Reina had killed the one man I loved, I was angry that the only woman I ever knew as my mother was my goddamn sister, that my own fucking birth mother gave me up so that she could continue living her rich lifestyle with her fucking pedophile husband. I was angry that our mother allowed her husband to repeatedly rape my sister. I was angry that so many muthafuckas had some sort of part in playing me. I was angry because I was weak.

I was angry and they would pay, all of them, even if it I had to die to do it. They would pay.

19 REVENGE

On the drive back to the house I started thinking about what Reina had used to poison me, but then it hit me. I had missed my period.

It all started to make sense, the nausea, fainting, vomiting. It could not have come at a better time, I just needed to make sure.

I pulled off on the next exit and headed toward the neighborhood Walmart. I searched hurriedly through the isles in search of a pregnancy test. I finally found it located near the sanitary napkins.

I rushed to the line and paid for it. It was no way that I was going to wait until I was back at the house to find out. I asked an associate where the restroom was located and headed toward it.

When I got in the restroom I read the directions on the box, pulled down my pants and pissed on the stick, concentrating so I wouldn't get any pee on the window part.

I sat the test on the napkin disposal in the stall and I waited. It wasn't even two minutes before the line appeared to indicate the test was done correctly. A minute later another line to form a plus.

Fuck, I'm pregnant with TJ's baby!

I slipped the test in my purse, headed out the stall to wash my hands and out of the bathroom toward the door to exit the store.

I was numb. There were no feelings of fear, happiness, sadness, nothing. It was a numbness that I had never felt.

When I got in the car I called TJ.

"Hello?" the piece of shit answered.

"Hey, I need to see you" I told him "where are you?"

"I'm at the clinic handling business" he replied.

"I'll meet you at the East Parlor, twenty minutes" I said before I hung up.

I headed toward the East Parlor forming my plan in my head. That would be the last time anyone would ever play me like a fool. I was going to show everybody just who they were fucking with and what I was capable of and they could thank Reina for that.

I was about to introduce them to a monster.

When I arrived at the East Parlor I was greeted by the one of the distros. "Park the car" I said as I handed him the keys and walked into the clinic. He was clearly surprised at my lack of greeting which he wasn't used to.

I escorted myself through the parlor and to my private suite. Once in, I picked up the phone and advised that I wanted a double desert when my guest arrived. Then I undressed to show just my hot pink lace panties and bra. I let my hair down and waited for TJ to arrive.

After about ten minutes, he walked in and was clearly pleasantly surprised when he saw me.

Before he could close the door to the suite I walked over to him half naked and licked his lips, then I licked his ear and after that his neck. While I was licking his ear I ran the palm of my hand down the front of his pants where I could feel his dick finding an erect position and I moaned a little to let him know that I felt it.

It drove him crazy when I moaned. He picked me up to carry me toward the couch and I saw the deserts being served. Both girls were gorgeous, but one stood out.

She was light skinned with green eyes and multiple tattoos that formed a mule on her body. She was particularly petite and had long straight hair. She had her hair pinned up in a high ponytail that displayed the beginning of her extensive butterfly vine work that covered her entire body.

Her bronzed skin made the colors on the work vivid as if she were a portrait. She had plump titties that sat up by themselves with a flat belly and a small round botty.

Her pussy had no hair, like it had been waxed and I was instantly turned on the moment I laid eyes on her. I wanted her.

When TJ sat me on the couch I motioned for her to come to me. When she walked over I leaned over and kissed her on her soft lips. She was very timid which was even more appealing.

"Have you ever been with a woman?" I asked her intrigued by her shock and timid look from my kiss.

TJ moved my panties to the side and started fingering me softly while I spoke to her.

"No Madam, but I'm here to serve you" she answered in a sweet innocent voice.

I moved TJ's hand and I got down from the top of the couch. I took her hand and helped her on to the couch to take my place where I was sitting.

"What makes you feel good?" I asked her.

"I'm here to serve you Madam" she responded and I smiled at her.

"Suck on her titties" I told TJ as I continued to smile at her. TJ started to softly suck on one of her titties and she began to loosen up.

I spread her legs open kneeled down in front of her and licked her pussy. She gave such an intense moan that my pussy wet up and I licked her again, searching for her clit. I licked her pussy like I missed it while TJ sucked her titties passionately.

She pushed down on my tongue and it drove me wild. I inserted my index and middle finger into her pussy while I licked her clit softly and passionately and she pushed up and down again my fingers and my tongue. She groaned in pleasure and leaned her head back while lifting her bottom searching for more.

Her breathing intensified and the volume of her moans became louder. She tried to push away but I fingered her harder and sucked her clit. She lost herself in her pleasure and my mouth filled with the sweet juices of her pleasure.

I pulled my fingers out of her and I tongue kissed TJ to share the sweetness of her cum while I unbuttoned his shirt and pants, pulling them off so hard that I ripped several buttons.

He positioned me next to the girl and I pushed her shoulder to slide her down the couch to the floor so that she was positioned with her face on front of TJ's dick. Then I stood up for him and he pulled my panties off and begin to passionately lick my pussy while she sucked on his dick.

He moaned from the pleasure she was giving him and I moaned from the feeling of his soft tongue. He inserted his index and middle finger into my ass as he was eating my pussy and I groaned of excitement.

I motioned the other dessert over to and pulled her on to the couch to suck on my titties. She sucked them perfectly and I grabbed her head as TJ provided immense pleasure to my pussy with his tongue.

I found myself caught up in the pleasure of the warmth of his tongue to my clit and I began to rock into his mouth while beginning to pull the hair of the dessert from all the excitement I was feeling.

TJ let out a groan of pleasure because the rock caused his dick to immense into the throat of his pleasure and she let out a slight choking sound.

Just then I felt an overwhelming urge to hold on to a heightened sensation that over took my body and I grabbed his head pushing it into my pussy fiercely and holding it so that he could not move at all.

I climaxed to the highest point and filled his mouth with the sensual juices that he so eagerly searched for. I could tell from his jolt of surprise that my body had given more cum in his mouth than he'd ever experienced. He was overwhelmed by the juices that filled his mouth and leaked intensely from his face.

He pulled his dick from the mouth of the first desert and flipped me over on the couch and stuck his dick in me aggressively. The look on his face was more than adequate to show that he was pleased with the extreme wetness that my pussy provided him.

He fucked me while the deserts kneeled on the side of the couch watching, waiting for a directive to move. But I let him have be to himself.

He moaned in intense pleasure, licking my nipples, and kissing my neck as he repeated the moving of his dick in and out of my pussy and I watched him.

He enjoyed it so much that he was lost in pleasure and didn't notice me watching him without cease.

The pleasure overcame him and he started speaking a language of an intense pleasure that reminded me of Pig Latin before he let his cum fill me up inside.

As his dick softened he fell on me in exhaustion and I nodded for the desserts to prepare the cleaning utensils.

They both exited the room for a few moments, before returning with the cleaning supplies.

I moved TJ off me and allowed them to clean my pussy of the mess. While they were cleaning, two other entrees joined the room and began to sanitize the areas around where we had enjoyed each other.

When they were done with me, they cleaned TJ while he lie on his back with his eyes closed. I dressed myself while he was being cleaned while watching him intently.

After his cleaning was complete, he opened his eyes and looked at me with a smile. I smiled back at him, but definitely not for the reason he was smiling.

He was happy, satisfied. I was about to snatch that shit right out of his hand.

"What?" he asked, curious about why I was smiling?

"What, what?" I asked him, acting like I didn't know why he was asking me such a weird question.

"Summer, you're smiling. It's been a long time since I've seen you smile like that" he said.

I just shrugged and walked over to him where I took a seat. I grabbed his hand and he lifted mine to kiss it.

"Can I ask you a question?" I asked him.

"You can ask me anything" he replied.

"Will you help me kill Reina?" I asked him sternly.

"Whatever you need me to do, I'm here for you" he said.

"Well, that's good. I was worried that you'd be hesitant to kill your sister" I replied casually.

TJ was silent, it was the first time that I'd ever seen him nervous. He fidgeted uncomfortably and scrambled around in his brain for something to say.

"I mean, I'm sure you would benefit from it just as much as I would, considering the fact that you both are planning to kill me."

Silence. TJ looked like he had seen a ghost. I could tell that he was debating on whether to strangle me or make a run for the exit.

"I see you're at a loss for words, so I'll just help make this decision for you. We're going to have a baby. I don't think Reina will like that very much, especially considering that your job was to keep me under control."

Nothing. He was still quiet. He didn't blink. He adjusted and readjusted his body on the couch as if something were sticking him.

"I found out that I was pregnant after I went to see my sister, Maddy. At first I thought Sydney had poisoned me, but then I realized, I hadn't gotten a period so I went to the store and grabbed a test" I told him as if we were engaging in a normal conversation.

"The cat was out of the bag when I heard Sydney's last name Tyson. Did you not think I'd put 2 and 2 together? I know you both think you had me fooled and that was a part of my plan."

"But this baby changes things for me, for us. We're going to take over your sister's business, after we kill her" I finished.

TJ cleared his throat, but even as his words came out the nervousness could still be heard. "Summer, Syd made me go along with it. I didn't want to hurt you, or even be involved" he started.

"TJ, save your bullshit. I don't want to hear it and I'm sick of the lies" I said firmly. "You were a willing participant and I'm not concerned with it. If you won't help me kill Sydney, then I'll kill your baby. Choose" I told him matter of factly.

"I'll do it. Please, don't hurt my baby Summer. That's a part of me growing in side of you. It's the only blood family I have if what you're saying is true."

I got up, walked over to my purse and pulled the pregnancy test from it. I handed it to him.

"What I'm saying is very true" I told him while handing it to him.

"When?" he asked me with total submission.

"She needs to die soon" I told him. "Once she finds out I'm pregnant, she will want to kill me."

"Ok, how do you want to do it?" he asked.

I laid out the plan for him, explaining to him that I was going to tell Reina that I was pregnant and the scenarios that would likely happen. I didn't plan to tell Reina the baby was TJ's but to leave the assumption that it could have been Ro's baby. I had never told her that TJ was the only one I'd ever fucked without a condom and I knew that she would assume that it was Ro's baby.

The anger would overwhelm her strategy and that is what I depended on. It was the only way to win. Reina was far too smart and if she was thinking clearly there would be no way to fool her, even with TJ's help.

When I was done with TJ I was going to kill him and bury him next to his sister, and then his baby. For the first time I was in the winner's chair for real.

We headed out the parlor, TJ following behind me like a wet puppy, grasping at my every command. In this position he reminded me of Ro and a part of me wanted to feel sorry for him, but I knew I couldn't.

This was the same man that planned to kill me. He had spent so much time plotting with that crazy bitch Reina and had ended up being in the worst position.

When we got to my car he opened the door for me. I seated myself in the car and looked out at him.

"Summer, I just want to say that I'm sorry, for everything" TJ said to me.

I grabbed the door handle from on the side of him and closed the car door in his face.

I started up the car and pulled off.

He was sorry?! Who really gives a fuck? I know he didn't think I did. It was evident that he realized that he'd lost control and was desperate to do whatever he could to get it back.

I headed to the house. As I was driving I dialed Reina's number.

"Hello?" she asked in an unusual tone of uncertainty. The only assumption was that TJ had already spoken to her. I was certain that he had told her about the baby, but I wasn't sure if he had told her my plan.

It was only one way to find out.

"Hi Rei, are you home? I have some exciting news to share with you!" I said in the most exciting voice that I could muster up.

"Yea, I'm here. I'll see you soon" she said as she hung up the phone.

She knows and she's not happy.

It gave me even greater pleasure to know. I was going to need some help so I put in a call to an old friend.

"Trice, hi, it's Summer."

I told Trice everything and gave her the portion of the plan that I needed her for.

I needed Trice because Reina wanted her badly. Many times when I would have Trice I'd come back and tell her about it. I'd describe the fucking in great detail and Reina would be excited.

She told me she wanted Trice, but I wouldn't let her have her. Trice was something that I kept for myself and Reina knew that Trice would not pleasure her unless I told her to. Trice was in love with me.

Reina's desire for Trice was going to give me the advantage. Trice was damn near irresistible.

When I finally pulled up to the house I saw that Trice was already awaiting my arrival. When she saw me step out of the car she walked over to meet me.

She was dressed in an all-black Moschino jumper that was sheer at the top. The jumper had a made on waist belt that was black with white lettering that read Moschino all the way around.

She didn't have on a bra and had nothing covering her nipples. The jumper provided a full view of her perfect perky titties.

Her jumper was accompanied by some white open toe Jimmy Choos that complimented her long legs.

Her hair was pulled back in a long fish tail braid with light strands falling down.

She wore a smoky eye with a red lip and she looked beautiful. Her dark skin glistened from the moisturizer that she used and she smelled of Chanel No 5 perfume.

Trice had exceeded my expectations and I knew that it would be easy for her with Reina. As a matter of fact, I counted on it.

She made my pussy wet the moment I laid eyes on her so I knew that she would do the same for Reina.

I grabbed Trice's hand and walked beside her on the way to the door of the house.

When I opened the front door I could see that Reina was waiting in the library drinking tea as she normally did.

"Reina?" I called out for her.

She came out the library and the minute she saw Trice she lit up like a firecracker.

"Rei, you know Trice! I thought I'd bring her as part of the celebration for the news I want to share" I told her.

Reina didn't take her eyes off Trice as I was talking.

She's right where I need her to be!

"Rei! I'm going to have a baby!" I screamed in excitement.

Reina turned from Trice to me and her facial expression told me that she had no idea. TJ hadn't spoken to her.

She was totally stunned by the news. "And, as a celebration, I thought I'd give you a treat" I continued as if I didn't even notice her shocked expression.

Trice walked over and took her hand leading her toward the stairwell.

Reina didn't say anything. She followed Trice in silence.

"Enjoy Trice and enjoy your treat Aunt Rei!" I said.

It must have thrown her off because she stopped and turned to look at me.

"What do you mean? Why are you calling me that?" she asked nervously.

"Rei, we've been friends for years, you're more like my sister and going to raise this baby to call you Auntie" I said.

"By who?" Reina asked.

"It's a long story. I think I've been pregnant for a while and didn't know it. I wasn't expecting it, but it's definitely a blessing! This baby will be the legacy that lives on!" I told her.

"Go, enjoy your gift, we'll talk later!" I said giving her the biggest smile ever.

For the first time I saw Reina vulnerable. She was confused, maybe upset, and nervous. It was clear that she had just received confirmation that her plan was fucked up.

Trice tugged Reina's arm to continue leading her upstairs and Reina complied.

I watched as they walked upstairs imagining what kind of pleasure Trice was about to give Reina.

Once they had disappeared from the stairwell I headed upstairs toward my room to call TJ and get the plan in motion.

When I reached the end of the hall that had the exit to my bedroom's wing, I heard a loud noise comparable to a powerful firecracker, and I spun around to see what it was.

That's when I saw her drop to the floor slowly, blood running out of her mouth, and a tear from her eye as she grasped for air and reached out to me.

I ran over to her in panic and my heart dropped to the floor. I picked up the phone and hit send to call the last number I had called.

I heard TJ answer. "Hello?" "Summer?"

I screamed in terror, "She killed her, she killed Trice!", and I could hear TJ screaming my name.

"Summer, I'm on my way!" he screamed. But I knew that he would be too late. When he arrived, I'd be there, probably dead with his baby lying next to Trice.

"Summer, why don't you go ahead and hang the phone up" Reina said in a voice that I had never heard before.

I pressed end on the call and looked up and suddenly I was looking into the barrel of a black 9MM, Reina at the other end of it.

ABOUT THE AUTHOR

Queen is a newly established author to the urban erotica world. She was previously in the magazine industry and has always been an avid reader. Queen primarily tailors her reads to the urban audience and enjoys losing herself in the fictional world to bring excitement and feelings to her readers.

Made in the USA
Middletown, DE
20 November 2020